Praise for <u>GRIND YOU</u>

"The brilliance of it all is breathtaking; literally, the most masterful climax and conclusion—I have never read its equal.

He writes like a man possessed. As if the very story you're reading has somehow taken over Day's being and poured itself out onto the page. I don't know if Nicholas Day sold his soul at a crossroads to bring us *Grind Your Bones to Dust* but this book feels like a pact made with the Devil to bring us the finest horror has to offer."

-Cemetery Dance, Sadie Hartmann

"Nicholas Day hooks you with a perfect trifecta of action, atmosphere, and character, setting you up like a pin in a bowling alley, only to mow you down with a perfect strike.

Grind Your Bones to Dust is a symphony of violence rendered with a poet's eloquent finesse and a madman's ecstasy, a full frontal assault to the senses and a testament to the abilities of a master craftsman."

-InkHeist, Shane Douglas Keene

"With *Grind Your Bones to Dust*, Day takes us on a tense journey down a dark, desolate road. And the lights are out. Veer too much to one side and we are rewarded with unapologetic violence, both natural and supernatural. Pull to the other side and we experience the full range of human emotion through the eyes of wonderfully vivid characters, including one man gripped by madness and another who is haunted by it. And it isn't our hands on the steering wheel. All we can do is sit back, put our faith in our guide, and enjoy the ride. The perfect blend of character, voice and setting, *Grind Your Bones to Dust* is cause for celebration; as is an author whose tremendous ability as a storyteller is only growing with every publication."

-This Is Horror, Thomas Joyce

"*Grind Your Bones to Dust* is very well-written and it is very, *very* dark. This book made me hurt for Nicholas Day, because it's so painfully raw in the truth it tells about the world and the chastisement it lays out for those who really believe God is listening. Day's writing etches his stories onto your mind in angry, bleeding strokes. *Grind Your Bones to Dust* might disgust you, will probably disturb you, and will burrow into the recesses of your mind. I loved it, but damned if I didn't need a drink afterwards."

-*Sci-Fi & Scary*, Lilyn George

"*Grind Your Bones to Dust* is a visceral, unapologetic, and unforgettable beast of a book. Nicholas Day utilizes haunting, poetic prose between each vicious scene with impressive skill. The cast of characters are strange, wild, and emote a realm of pain that hooks you into their lives and refuses to let you go. Day spins us a world where the monstrous donkeys eat flesh and the characters embark on Godless quests, but the horrific sermon of human brutality is what will stay with you long after the book is closed. Say a prayer if you like, but no salvation or redemption will bother to save you from what Day has in store…"

-Sara Tantlinger, Bram Stoker Award-winning author of
The Devil's Dreamland

"Holy demon donkeys! *Grind Your Bones to Dust* reads like Tarantino's *Hateful Eight* if it had been written by William S. Burroughs on some modern-day synthetic…yet as much as it punches right into your guts, it manages to grab you by the heart with that same fist…and twist. What makes Day distinctive among the bizarro tribe is that he manages to load up his amazingly bent imagination with emotional payoff, chapter after chapter. Quick-paced and nasty, this book bends genres as easy as rubber prison bars, proving beyond a doubt that Nicholas Day is a strong-arm writer to be reckoned with, and establishes him firmly among the ruling authors of contemporary Bizarro Horror."

-Michael Arnzen, Bram Stoker Award-winning author of
Grave Markings and *Licker*

Praise for Nicholas Day

NOBODY GETS HURT AND OTHER LIES

"*Nobody Gets Hurt and Other Lies* is a fantastic collection. Nicholas Day is a writer with undeniable talent."

- Hellnotes, Elaine Pascal

AT THE END OF THE DAY I BURST INTO FLAMES

"Existential poetry in the form of a horror story—I mean, a love story. *At the End of the Day I Burst into Flames* is like a having a smoke—killing you, intoxicating you, connecting you to just how quickly it all burns away. Beautiful, sad, on fire."

-Laura Lee Bahr, Wonderland Award-winning author of *Haunt* and *Angel Meat*

"He doesn't shy away from the difficult moments and bares everything like a confession of sin or declaration of devotion; every page, passage, sentence, is musical."

-This Is Horror, Thomas Joyce

NOW THAT WE'RE ALONE

"Hauntings, psychosis, man-eating turtles and G.G. Allin in space, sign me up! *Now That We're Alone* displays Nicholas Day's ability to straddle multiple genres and make each story feel believable. He has an imagination that is as limitless as his talent. It's dark, horrific and beautiful, with a blend of otherworldly terror and heartbreakingly human trauma that creates a must read collection."

-Michelle Garza, co-author of Bram Stoker Award-nominated novel, *Mayan Blue*

"Often horrific, relentlessly stark, and truly unforgettable."
-Kirkus Reviews

NECROSAURUS REX

"Nicholas Day is a fantastic writer, he's a thrilling, poetic, gruesome and balls to the wall in-your-face craftsman of twisted horror and bizarro."

- *SCREAM Magazine*, Jonathan Reitan

"There is not a misplaced word in all of the book, everything is working together to tell this story. As long as a reader goes in with an open mind and a tolerance for the absolutely disgusting and the absolutely beautiful, Necrosaurus Rex delivers. With more content and character than a thousand pages of your average book, author Nicholas Day has achieved something amazing, something you have to experience to understand."

-*Hellnotes*, Tim Potter

Grind Your Bones to Dust

Nicholas Day

Excession Press

First edition published by Excession Press, 2019
www.excessionpress.com

ISBN: 978-1-7339901-3-4

Printed in the United States

This book is dedicated to those who would reduce this world to a massive grave and create a Hell for the living.

I hate you.

PART ONE

Louis ran through the dark because he did not want to die screaming while being torn apart and eaten alive. Not like dear Elliot, whose high-pitched terror roared through the night like a train on its way to Hell. And Louis wept when he realized it was his name Elliot shrieked into the pitch.

But he didn't dare stop running.

The desert air chilled Louis. He wore no shirt, just a pair of long woolen underwear. Only one of the three milk glass buttons had been fastened. Sheer terror set hard and fast and made dressing a distant second to surviving. His labored breath the only sound heard over the rush of air as he kept his harried pace. Unseen flora, rock, and dry detritus pierced the bottoms of his feet. There'd been no time for putting on shoes. Not after what he'd seen.

Or, what had seen him.

Elliot had been screaming before Louis jolted awake. No moonlight. Lamplight blew out before they retired.

Some kind of large beast had hold of Elliot's shoulder and Elliot beat his fist against the creature. Louis reached out but flinched as something grunted just outside the hole torn in the side of their tent. A second animal lurched inside and snapped at Elliot's hand, raking enough skin off the thumb and index finger to expose bone. He screamed and reached out to Louis but the two creatures yanked Elliot from the tent and dragged him into the nothing, no matter how hard he kicked, no matter how hard he yelled.

As if sound and fury could stop what was coming.

Louis fumbled in the dark for his clothes but only managed the long underwear when Elliot screamed in such a way that logic ceased. Louis acted no longer as one gearing up for a fight, but found himself reduced to one animal listening to the slaughter of its own. He scrambled out of the tent. Their horses were gone. He peered in the direction of Elliot's panicked shrieking. Shadows spilled over themselves, like looking to the bottom of a deep lake and imagining the movement of strange creatures.

Four dark shapes lumbered in the darkness and seemed to circle around a terrified Elliot. One of those shapes hunched over and Louis heard the unmistakable sound of meat pulling from bone. Elliot cried like a child. The other two shapes seemed to titter and sway, excited by Elliot's distress, and then, to Louis's utter mortification, someone in the dark whispered his name.

Louis.

And Louis trembled. His breathing seized.

One of the shapes faced him. The obsidian glint of the beast's eyes shone like a wet lacquer. A guttural snort preceded a shattering two-toned bray. Goosebumps flooded Louis's arms and his legs. His body shook as a tremor before an earthquake.

And in the next instant, Louis knew he ran for his life, though he did not yet know where he ran to, because instinct had taken over. He was a mind floating inside a machine programmed to survive. His body knew where to go even if his consciousness hadn't quite figured it out.

The previous day, Elliot and Louis had ridden horseback past a meager homestead while they surveyed a stretch of land that was to become part of a great highway, stretching from northern Nevada and across the southeast of Oregon, all the way to the sea. President Dwight D. Eisenhower had signed the Federal-Aid Highway Act not a few years prior, and communities off the beaten path felt the urge to tap into the black veins being laid across every U.S. state. Surveying was in high demand, and the job paid well, or at least well enough to support a family. It was also a position which kept one *away* from family for long stretches, which had its own merits.

Louis ran to that meager homestead. A couple miles jaunt, for sure, but there were no other homes, nowhere to take shelter. In fact, that place had been the only residence in sight for the last two days. Otherwise, Louis would have to run all the way to Adel, some fifty-odd miles. And if he went that far, he may as well keep running until he got back home to Klamath Falls.

He knew he would never make it to Adel. Making the distance to the homestead would be victory enough. He could only pray that he'd be able to see home again, to see sweet Ruth's smile and hear young Danny's laugh. Who would protect them if he were to die?

The thought of either of them coming to harm hardened his resolve and he pushed through exhaustion into something like a trance. His arms and legs warmed and breathing eased. He ran to the homestead, yes, but in his mind he ran to them.

Louis didn't know what had attacked Elliot, but it couldn't possibly be worse than what was looking for Ruth and Danny. A nightmare walked the earth, a monstrous being who only knew pain and how to inflict it. Louis had always been able to protect them, moving them when needed, taking jobs that allowed for a transient life.

His brother, James, would kill them all if he found them.

And so, Louis ran through the dark. Love gave him the strength. Fear showed him the way. No harm would come to them. He would never allow that, not as long as he lived.

The desert remained a cold and scheming stillness, despite his rapid heartbeat and sharp breaths. Silence stalked the mind as surely as any nocturnal creature in this vast nothing. Louis remembered being a small boy in the bath and holding his head under the water. Eyes open, of course, then and now. The sensation identical, a detached calm washed over him. He imagined himself a creature at the bottom of murky water, and wondered who or what may be looking down upon him.

Louis was not a believer. Those customs had not been part of his youth. And the birth of James undoubtedly begged the question of a loving God's existence. All that, to say nothing of Louis's own heart, itself an aberration to the church where Ruth and Danny prayed. Louis wondered if any members of the congregation suspected him, or if it even mattered at all.

He could not bring himself to pray, though he would hope against hope that James would never find them, that he would forget them, that he would die.

The smell of burning wood singed his nostrils and filled his lungs. In that familiar scent a promise of warmth endured. Fire burned, yet unseen, as a salvation. The homestead couldn't be far. A glow, in the distance, but the relief quickly changed to renewed panic.

Something ran—galloped—from behind. Whatever killed Elliot now raced toward Louis. The once-distant glow grew in brilliance. He could make it to the homestead. He had to make it.

Louis tried to yell but choked on his own dry throat. He swallowed, hard, and took as deep a breath as he could muster. And his terror bellowed out of him.

"Help me," he screamed. "Please, help me!"

The fire was not inside the home but at the edge of the property, a good-sized bonfire that lit up the immediate surroundings in a wash of deepest orange and streaks of white and yellow. Beyond the fire sat the home, and further yet stood the barn, like a black obelisk. The crackle and burn of wood, the soft rumble of consuming flame. He took another deep breath.

"They're coming! They're after me!"

Louis ran past the fire and towards the house. He collapsed onto the porch and rolled to his back. The front door wrenched open and the iron hinges sang into the night. Light crept across the porch where he lay.

"Thank you," Louis said. "Thank you, Jesus."

Louis looked up to see his savior, but all that stared back were the two deep, dark eyes of a double-barreled shotgun. Louis reached out weakly. He smiled.

"Thank you," he said through delirium.

Then, Louis drifted into unconsciousness and the shotgun went back inside the house. What roamed through the dark, beyond the fire, stayed in the dark. The bonfire kept vigil till sunrise, and it began to smolder as cool air burned away and shadows retreated.

A rooster crowed from atop the home.

Louis woke. He rose to his feet and vomited over the porch railing, then fell back to his knees. He kept hold of the rail, hung his head, and sobbed. Elliot's last words had been his name. And Louis ran away. The sound of meat tearing from bone crept out of the darkest recesses of his memory.

He cried harder than before, shattering the silence of the desert like a rock through glass. His chest ached. He could no longer breathe. Someone placed a hand against his back but exhaustion robbed Louis of any proper reaction.

"Breathe," the homesteader said. "Use this. Get ahold of yourself."

The old man held out a tattered shirt. Louis took it, held it to his face and breathed deep. In a few minutes, he managed to regain his composure. He then used the shirt to wipe his eyes. Another minute or two passed before he could face the man with any kind of dignity. Louis had spent his whole life hiding his emotions. Crying in front of anyone, let alone a stranger, was worth a whipping from his old man. A belt and a fist were persuasive teachers. Indignation swelled in that memory and Louis directed his ire at the man before him.

"You left me out here?"

"Goddamned right I did. Half-naked and screaming like a banshee." The homesteader hitched a thumb towards the front door. "I got a woman and a child in there."

"I could've been killed."

The old man stepped off the porch. "Well, you weren't." He gazed at the smoking debris at the edge of the property. "Besides, they don't care much for the fire. Keeps 'em away, most nights."

"What the hell are they?"

"I know what they look like, but I can't rightly say what they *are*."

"Couldn't see anything last night. Thought they might be bears."

"Nah." The old man spit. "Buncha feral ass."

A loud bark of a laugh escaped Louis.

The homesteader looked over his shoulder. "I didn't say nothing funny."

"You mean to tell me that I—that my partner, my *friend*—that we were attacked by donkeys? That he was killed by damned donkeys?"

"Ayup."

"Pardon me, mister, but that's the craziest sonofabitchin' thing I ever heard."

"It surely ain't, feller, I promise you that."

Nothing steadied a man like the resolve that he could not be wrong. Louis found his footing and his balance. He stepped off the porch and joined the old farmer, though he kept a respectable distance.

"Not possible. I grew up around horses. Hell, my old man kept a donkey for years. They don't . . . those animals don't do that kind of thing. Bears do. Or maybe a couple big cats, like cougars or some kind of mountain lion."

The farmer turned, eyebrows raised and mouth curled into a smirk, clearly annoyed with the man before him. "Your daddy kept some horses. Well, good for you, son. But you ain't hearing me. I'm telling you I've seen them." The homesteader looked Louis up and down. He took in a deep breath and nodded as one does when the other party is set to disagree. "Look, you've had a helluva night. Let's get you cleaned up, get you some clothes, some food. After that, I'm gonna tell you a story. You'll either believe it or you won't. Makes no difference no how. They'll be back, tonight, just as sure as the sun. Me and the missus got chores. You help out, you can stay. Otherwise, Adel is that ways a spell."

"I'd never make it there before nightfall."

"Not without a horse."

"You telling me you got horses?"

"Telling you I got one horse. I need her, today. You stick around and we can ride out to Adel first thing, tomorrow."

"First thing?"

"Ayup."

Louis held out his hand. The homesteader accepted the gesture and shook with a strength that stunned Louis. Skin like tree bark and a grip like hard earth, the old man was practically the embodiment of the land surrounding them.

"Name's Thomas," the old man said.

"Louis."

"Pleased to meet you, Louis. Wish it were under better circumstances." Thomas nodded, sauntered up the porch steps.

And Louis followed Thomas into the man's home.

A woman, much younger than Louis expected, and a small boy stood in front of the fireplace, perfectly still and wide-eyed. The two of them looked as though they'd been waiting like that their entire lives. Dirty faces, the both of them, but tanned to a degree that a little dirt didn't much matter. Skinny, too, like they'd taken the notion of working to the bone to heart.

A modest cross hung on the wall behind them like a guardian angel.

Oil lamps on the mantle place. A wood-burning stove at the back of the house in what served as a kitchen. Louis forgot people still lived like this, that he'd lived like this, and he hoped for the sake of the woman and child that Thomas was a better father than Louis had known. He'd always suspected that an abused heart recognized its own, and he did not recognize this wife and child. Their fear was clearly of him, and for that Louis was grateful. He smiled at them.

They did not smile in return.

"Matthias, you go on and get some water. Hattie, we're letting this feller clean himself up a bit. He's going to borrow some of my clothes and help with the chores while I head out and get more wood for tonight's fire—"

Hattie shot a glare at Thomas that'd skin an animal and Thomas raised a hand and shook his head.

"He ain't gonna bother you none. We got work and he's a helping hand. And I best go on and get more wood 'cause we done burned our last stack, you hear? Besides, you can have the shotgun. He tries giving you any funny business, cut him down." Thomas looked to Louis for approval. "Sound fair to you, son?"

"Reckon I can live with that."

Thomas explained that he would be heading for a spot of trees due south and that the job tended to last a good chunk of the day, between cutting down what he needed and then hauling it back. But he swore he'd return well before sunset, and that the night's bonfire would be ready to go.

After Louis had his bath, Thomas handed him a pair of black slacks and a collared, white button-down shirt. Not a mirror in the house, so Louis had no choice but to look down at himself and imagine how he came across.

"You always dress this fancy for chores?" Louis asked.

"Only if you think going to church is a chore."

"There's a church out here?"

"Used to be one."

"Not enough people, I reckon."

"Not enough God. Hell, son, pretty sure He's never stepped foot in Oregon no how, let alone the rest of it. No matter where you go, though, folk just keep building churches hoping He'll finally show up. But He never do, and that's real salt in the wound for some people. Make an otherwise decent man angry and wild. Get wild enough, man stops quoting scripture and starts lashing out, making threats, setting fires and such. Hurt his own. Man may as well be a rabid animal at that point. You ever put down something rabid, Louis?"

"No, sir, can't say I have."

"Lot a men tell you there's no pride in it. Truth is, 'bout nothing in the world fill you with more pride than protecting yours. Cut a beast down that's gunning for your family and you may as well be God."

"How come you never, you know"—Louis motioned towards the outside—"cut *them* down?"

Thomas walked across the room. He put his hands to either side of the window and looked about the colorless expanse. His fingertips blanched to a color of pearl as he pressed against the wall. He let a small laugh but kept still, addressing Louis without looking at him.

"I promised you a story, but I guess I owe you two of 'em. First one my granddaddy told me when I was little. Second one happened to me a couple months back. But I think we ought to head outside, as I don't want the little one listening in."

Small steps, just outside the door to the room and out of sight, hurried away. The moment proffered a bit of levity and Louis could not help but smile. The older man was nothing if not intimidating, but his obvious love of the woman and the boy made Louis feel as though he were as safe as they, if only by association. Thomas beckoned, and both men walked together towards the two-story barn, which sat a stone's throw away from the modest home.

Thomas used his boot to kick up a latch at the bottom of the barn door and then used both hands to pull it open, walking it back slowly, hinges cracking and popping like some distant thunder. The air from inside smelled of moist earth and dry hay and horse manure. A small hint of cool humidity seemed to leech through the heavy stench, which felt alien to the arid landscape. Thomas took a deep breath and patted his sides. He smiled and winked at Louis.

"Built this barn around a well. Deep sonofabitch, like looking into the heart of the Earth. It was here when I claimed the land. Easy enough to miss, too, especially if you're on horseback. A hole's a hole out here, you know, and best to be avoided. Snake bites or a broke leg's about all they're good for."

"Can't imagine it was easy to find."

"Well, I didn't find it, never would have but for an Indian feller—Modoc, or some such—passing through here on the way back to the reservation. Needed water for the last leg of the trip. Asked me if I minded him using our well, and laughed his fool head off when I told him the nearest water was a couple miles yonder. Then, he showed me what had been right under my nose the whole time. Goddamned well is what kept us here the last two years. Otherwise, we might have moved on. Saved ourselves a lot of trouble."

"How long have the, uh, you know—the critters—how long they been around?"

"About two months of aggression. I'd seen 'em, in the distance, a handful of times before but, yeah, off and on this whole spring. I'd kill them if I could find them but they stick to the night, now, and don't seem to leave much track, not that I was ever a very good hunter. Anyway, you help me around the barn a minute, hitch up this cart and I can make way. Promised you a couple stories, anyhow."

Louis learned that Thomas had been an only child, his father an American of German descent and his mother a Greek immigrant. The couple married in the summer of 1895. Thomas showed up in the winter of 1900. They lived in Southern Illinois, and during that time, Thomas's maternal grandfather yet lived. The elderly man couldn't do much besides tell stories, and young Thomas eagerly listened. Some of them were about the old man's youth, wild stories of derring-do which Thomas's mother oft denied as outright lies, at best. At worst, she felt grandfather's stories to be in poor taste for an impressionable boy. And as Thomas relayed this to Louis, the old farmer grinned enough that his eyes all but disappeared, likely remembering some bit of mischief inspired by his long-deceased relative. Louis smiled in return, and wished his own memories brought him any amount of joy, but his mind wandered back into the darkness of his own youth. He thought of his brother, James, and the smile was struck from his face.

Thomas seemed to take note and cleared his throat, letting his own smile dim while he pointed to the cart saddle hanging on the back wall of the barn, flanked by all manner of tools meant to rend and hew the earth and its increase. A chopping block, stained by blood, sat on the floor below, itself framed by an array of chicken feathers. A cursory glance revealed no hatchet.

Louis lifted the cart saddle off its hook and then passed it over the side of the stable to Thomas. The horse acted skittish and Thomas spoke in a hush as he stroked the animal's neck. He assured Louis that she simply wasn't used to strangers but would calm down before too long. Then, in the next moment, Thomas spoke to Louis in much the same tone. The story, he said, had been told to him by his grandfather, meant to scare him, a punishment for his own mistreatment of a gelding.

"Pappous talked a lot about the old country and he knew more stories than you could shake a stick at, but that particular story's been sticking with me a whole lot of late. Way he told it was that a king on the Black Sea owned a quartet of man-eating horses, and that the Greeks sent their man Hercules to go and get 'em. But he didn't go alone. Had a party of folks, warrior-types that went along with him. And they show up and they get the horses but this king, see, he's not terribly happy to see his prized beasts go, so there's a big ol' battle, as men do, and while everybody's killing each other over these horses, Hercules tells his sidekick, Thomas—and this is the part where the old man liked to embellish, 'cause sure as shit wasn't no ancient Greek Thomases. Anyway, he tells Thomas to look after and protect the animals, and Thomas is brave but foolish. He agrees to watch over the horses . . . but he keeps his back to them. He's expecting the king's men. What he doesn't expect is the damned horses.

"They kick out his knees, first, and when he tries crawling they crush his arms. The four beasts strip him naked and keep kicking at him until bones start poking through his skin and eventually there's no fight left in Thomas, except to cry for help, but there's a battle going so nobody hears him. And don't you know what that old man tells me next, that before those horses ate his face and eyes and guts, they bite his pecker off and eat his balls . . . while he's *alive*. The shit people tell a kid, I swear. Probably had nightmares about that for weeks, but forgot about it for well on forty-odd years. Until this year, till they showed up. Look here, now, I'll lead her out and into the yard. Grab that cart and wheel it on out. You can help me hitch her up. Seems plenty calm, now."

The cart was lighter than expected. The cracked, dry wood belied the cart's sturdy structure, and Louis imagined that the vehicle, like the house and barn, had been built by the man who waited in the yard. In that instant, Louis felt jealous of the man's wife and their son. Some folk were blessed while others were damned, and it took these chance encounters to know exactly where you stood in life. Louis might yet save Ruth and Danny but he knew that for him there would be no salvation. He was born damned.

"Louis, be as kind as to hand me that collar there in the back of the cart, please."

In his youth, Louis had watched his own father, Samuel, hitch a cart on several occasions, all the while cursing and swatting the animal until it cowed to his demands, submission through intimidation. How Samuel treated that horse is how he treated his sons and his wife. Nothing spoke louder than the man's hands. As the plow horse got older, all it took was the sound of the back door swinging open and the animal's eyes would be white and wild, its breath ragged, skin quivering. Living like that, one learns to like being alone. Approaching footsteps can raise a pulse. An opening door can seize a heart. Being around that kind of anger can feel like drowning. And all things are relative to a child, same as any other animal. Give them enough pain and fear and that's what they will come to expect. Some of them will even desire it, inflict it.

Or become it.

Many years now separated Louis from his father's trespasses and Samuel was long dead. Though, it felt to Louis as though the man were always just behind him, his hands balled into fists, his eyes red and watery. And now, before Louis stood a man who, in that moment, showed more care towards a horse than Louis ever knew as a child, save rare moments with his mother. Nothing quite opened those old wounds like seeing love and affection bestowed freely, as if they were gifts to be given away with no regard.

Thomas patted the horse and the animal gave him a nudge, then Thomas produced a bit of grain from a back pocket and fed it to the horse, patting the animal a second time. The collar and hames went on first, Thomas being as thoughtful enough to hold the collar upside down so as to give the animal's ears enough room to fit through without a squeeze, then turning it right side up once it was past the head. After that, Thomas buckled the cart saddle. Then, the bridle, the reins, the bit, and Thomas made as if to start talking but stopped when he looked up at his new charge.

Louis wiped his eyes, sucked back some snot, and looked away from Thomas.

Thomas studied the younger man for a moment and worked at his bottom lip before finishing the hitch, unsure as to whether or not it were wise to leave this broken man in the company of his kin. Hattie wouldn't stand for much nonsense, though, and she had always been a better shot than he. There'd been that mess, back in Illinois, and she stood her ground, then. And she fought off the preacher man, last winter, likely would've killed him herself had Thomas not arrived when he did. Thomas found it in himself to smile, again. Louis wouldn't stand a chance against Hattie, if it came to it. No reason not to continue being friendly, no reason not to tell one last story.

"Couple months back, I see all four of them up on that ridge, yonder. Stood so still I thought maybe I was just seeing things, rocks or trees or something. But, when I looked back, after chores and such, they were gone. Showed up, again, couple days later.

Same place, same formation as before. Then it got to where they were getting closer and closer to the house. I'd see them out there one minute and then they'd be off again to wherever it is they go. Now, at that time, we had a second horse and he liked to graze, so I'd get him out of the barn early and let him roam with the other animals out back. Pretty tame boy, never much worried about him tearing off or nothing. And that's all fenced in back there, anyway. So, he's set to roaming and I'm back in the barn when I hear him whinny something awful, and of course I come a running, but it's too damn late. Horse is deader than a doornail. Throat open, leg broke, skull cracked like an egg, brains running out in a puddle. There they were, those bastards, standing in the distance. I went and grabbed the gun but they were long gone. Rode out to where they'd been standing. Found what I first thought was a bit of offal, but it was my colt's balls. Heathens chewed them up and spit them out, like they wanted me to find them like that, like they were sending me some kind of warning—"

"But you didn't actually *see* them attack the horse."

"No, Louis, you're right, I didn't see 'em . . . that time. Couple weeks later, though, I get up early so I could ride up to Adel for some supplies and to deliver some post. I'm walking up to the barn when I glance over and notice all the animals huddled at the far back corner of the pen. I'm so fixated on them crowding together that it takes me a dozen strides or so before I see the problem. A donkey, black as a coalie's ass, had one of our goats pinned to the ground, goat's belly opened up, and that donkey just biting deeper and deeper.

"After a minute, the donkey raised its head. Blood up to its eyes, running out its nostrils and mouth, and it chewed and chewed. Watched me the whole time and never blinked once.

Eventually, the donkey dipped back in for seconds.

"I tell you, my feet were planted to the ground. Never seen anything like that in all my years. And I swear to God I hear my ol' pappous' voice, just as clear as a bell. First thing I think to do is hightail it for the barn and grab my hatchet. Just as I'm clearing the fence, that beast picks the carcass up and chucks it over the other side. His three friends trot up and start picking at the body. I brought that hatchet down, so help me, sunk it deep in the withers, not that you'd know it. Sonofabitch cleared that fence and they bolted."

"What did he say?"

"Not sure if I cotton to your meaning."

"You heard your grandfather say something."

"Oh, well, it was more like a whisper, really. Said my name and that was it."

"Damn."

The men exchanged exasperation and a few pleasantries before agreeing that it was due time for the patriarch to be on his way. Thomas suggested Louis wait out back for instruction from Hattie. And then he left.

The wheels of the cart made a shrill squeal as they turned and as the distance between the farm and cart grew, the sound took on the quality of birdsong, like a hawk's whistle. Louis watched the man and horse as they grew smaller, losing detail to distance and becoming hardly more than a hint of movement until they faded into the desert. A strange voice called out and the hair on the back of his neck stood on end.

Louis.

He spun around. Hattie stood in the pen behind the house, shotgun over her shoulder. She waved him over. Strangers with guns normally vexed him, but this was a welcome vision compared to what he had been expecting.

"You ever work a farm, mister?" Hattie asked.

"Yes, ma'am," Louis said. "One about the size of this, actually, a family farm. Cut my teeth on farm work. Not as many pigs, and no goats, but plenty of chickens."

"Simple yes or no would suffice. You're only here for the day."

"Tell me what needs done and I'll do it. May even take my time, that way we're out of each other's hair."

A smile, though gone in a blink, graced Hattie's face. She took the shotgun off her shoulder and let it hang at her side.

"Keep that attitude, mister, and we'll part on good terms."

Hattie directed Louis to the chicken feed and told him where to toss it and that shooing off the other animals would be necessary. Take your time, she insisted, more than once. A bucket, she explained, would be waiting by the backdoor. When he finished with the chickens, he'd need to milk the goats. She would take care of the trio of hogs. Potato patch needed watering, but could wait until care was taken of the animals.

Matthias usually found himself in charge of barn upkeep, but Hattie elected to leave that to Louis, as well. An extra hand in the house would be greatly appreciated and she looked forward to having extra time with the boy. Youth passed quickly, and she fretted that Matthias would soon enough be a memory, as she had become memory to her own kin.

"Once all that's done," Hattie said, "then you give that backdoor a knock, and we'll figure out what to do with you."

Hattie did not turn her back to Louis. She waited for him to make for the barn, and he heard the backdoor shut as he went about his own way. He didn't blame the woman. If the tables were turned, he doubted that he'd be any more trusting.

How often had trust been misplaced throughout history? After all, Elliot surely trusted Louis to come to his aid. Of course he did. For why else would he have screamed so? Louis weighed upon those last moments and how dreadful each second must have been, and he fought in vain to keep from polluting his own guilt with details from Thomas's grisly stories.

Louis fed the animals. The chickens were guarded and given time to feed. Goats were milked. Two trips to the well and the potato patch glistened in the shade of the barn, the ground darkened briefly before drinking deep the water. The desert seemed to swallow any sound except what existed between one's ears. Elliot's screams were as inescapable as the sun. After cleaning out the stable, Louis knocked twice at the backdoor, thought about that shotgun, and then made sure to step back into the yard.

But no gun greeted him, only Hattie. And she smiled. Her arms were crossed and she let her head tilt to the side. She walked out of the house and into the yard, inspecting the animals. Then, she went through the gate towards the potato patch and, after that, stepped into the barn before returning to Louis. She gave him an once-over, rubbing her chin with one hand while resting the other hand against her hip.

"Quicker than I expected. Got a good discipline about you. You fight in the war, Louis?"

"No, ma'am. Registered with Selective Service, classified 3-A."

"Wife and kids?"

"Yes, ma'am."

"I was young when I met Thomas. Still look like a girl, I suppose, but I wager I'm about your age. Wanted to get away from my folks and he didn't feel much like dying alone. That's how Matthias came to be. My family didn't approve, if I'm putting it kindly. That's how come we ended up out here."

"Thomas doesn't strike me as the type to run from trouble."

"Thomas never ran from nothing in his whole life. You don't run from happiness, you run to it. We're happy here, away from all the noise and the gossip. Nothing taking that away, you hear?"

"How many bonfires will it take to convince you otherwise?"

"They may be mean as Hell but they're just animals. All I need is a clear shot."

"Those animals . . . they tore my friend to pieces."

"And I believe you, mister, I surely do. But that is what man and animal been doing since the very beginning. What happened to your friend ain't nothing special, nothing that hasn't happened to a lot of other men. And women."

"That's a helluva thing to say to me."

"Only if you don't like hearing the truth. No, a *hell* of a thing—I'd say—is a man so detached from the world that he would levy surprise at the natural order of things . . ."

The last few words were spoken in a fade. Hattie pushed past Louis. She raised her hand above her brow, looking into the distance.

There was a ridge due west, maybe a quarter mile out, give or take. It had to be the ridge Thomas mentioned that morning. Louis raised his own hand and felt a chill run though his back. Elliot's screams roared within him and Louis trembled.

At that distance, the shapes were unrecognizable. Rocks, perhaps, or trees. Not a movement to tell you otherwise. But there were four of them.

"Hattie." Louis swallowed hard and cleared his throat.

"I see 'em," she said. "Louis, I want you to come stand next to me, you hear? Stand here and keep an eye on them. I'll be right back."

The gun had been loaded well before Thomas left her with the stranger. She reached up on the high shelf beside the back door and grabbed the box of cartridges. She'd missed her chance to put that preacher down. It'd be a damned shame if she were to miss taking out one—or, God willing, all—of these heathen beasts.

"Momma?"

Hattie looked across the room at Matthias. He stood, a bucket of soapy water in one hand and a sopping wet sponge in the other. The look on his face broke her heart. Guilt briefly supplanted her excitement.

"Nothing you need worry about, Matty. Keep at those windows. Me and Mister Louis are fixing to take care of an animal problem. You stay inside, I mean it, and you keep working."

The look on his face went unchanged until she raised her voice.

"I said get."

Matthias knew well enough to do as he was told.

Hattie hollered at Louis as she descended the back steps. "They still out there?'

Louis called out. "Yes, ma'am." And he never looked away from them, even when he heard the gate to the pen swing open and clack shut. After a minute, Hattie made her way around the front of the house and stood opposite Louis on the other side of the fence. Even then, his eyes remained trained on the animals in the distance.

"You're never gonna hit them from here," Louis said.

"Don't intend to hit 'em from here."

"Thomas wouldn't—"

Hattie grabbed Louis by the collar and he had no choice but to face her.

"Thomas wouldn't say a goddamned thing, mister. You understand me?"

Louis jerked away and looked back towards the ridge.

"Oh . . . oh, Jesus Christ." He quickly brought his hand to his mouth. "They're coming."

Hattie lifted the rifle before turning around, keeping her eyes on Louis long enough to holler one last demand of him. "Get inside. Keep Matthias safe."

Louis covered the distance, initially in a scramble but quickly became wide galloping strides. He cleared the small porch and slammed into the back door. The door wrenched open and he slammed it closed with his body weight. Dishes rattled and a frame jumped from the wall, shattering on the floor. Matthias stood, dumbstruck, across the room. The bucket lay on its side beside the boy. Soapy water spread across the floor in all directions, pooling in certain places while seeping between the floorboards in others. Louis raised a finger to his mouth, hushed the boy.

"G-go back in that room," Louis said. "Lock the d-door."

Matthias didn't wait for Louis to finish. The bedroom door slammed shut. A bolt snapped into place. Louis ran his hand across his face and pinched the bridge of his nose. He crawled to the nearest window, got to his knees, and raised his head just enough to peer out and over the wooden sill.

Hattie stood inside the enclosure, now. The dress she wore had torn at the hem. Fabric split all the way to her right knee. A bit of the material remained atop the fence where she had climbed over.

She carried herself like a seasoned hunter. Shotgun raised and rested against her shoulder. She rocked back and forth for a second to find the best balance. Her head positioned above the barrel so she could hone in on her line of sight.

Get them at the fence, she thought.

The four donkeys ran fast, much faster than any horse she had ever seen. They would not stop at the fence. Over, maybe, or through.

"Oh shit."

Their speed doubled, each animal a black freight train bearing down upon her. She fired. A spray of red misted the air but was quickly swallowed by the cloud of dust which rose in their wake. They did not stop.

She reloaded, took aim, and fired.

The animals were as a black cloud and a streak of blood like crimson lightning crackled across their countenance. A storm so close she could see its eyes. They sounded of thunder and the earth shook beneath her feet.

"I'm sorry, Matty."

Reload.

The lead animal left the ground and soared over the fence. The other three went straight through, brittle wood exploding in all directions.

Aim—

The beast slammed into Hattie on its descent, the butt of the shotgun met with enough force to dislocate her shoulder. A hoof across the face stifled an oncoming scream. Her upper lip split in half, teeth and blood dribbled down her chin and dress.

The donkeys circled Hattie. She tried to raise herself and screamed as the dislocated arm folded beneath her. She moaned.

23

The donkeys let out trill whinnies and atonal brays. They cackled, laughing like something out of a dark dream.

Hattie crawled. They bit into her arms. She screamed as two of them lifted her off the ground. A third circled behind and took hold of her long hair. She cried out and thrashed. Strands of hair pulled clean from her scalp. The donkey waited patiently and when she ceased her thrashing it leaned in a second time and got a better hold. She could not wrench free. The animal pulled down on its mouthful of hair, forcing Hattie to lean backwards.

The fourth donkey trotted around the front of her. It nipped at her dress. She tried to strike the animal with her boots but with her head pulled so far back, she could not see her target. The donkey turned away from her, kicked, and struck a blow against her knee.

Hattie's leg bent at an unnatural angle.

Inside the house, crying under his mother and father's bed, Matthias pressed his hands to his ears while Hattie shrieked outside.

She sunk in the animals' grip, her body racked with pain. Her chest heaved, once, then a second time. Vomit poured out of her mouth, down her face, and into her hair.

I have to do something, Louis thought. But what could he do?

The shotgun lay not five feet from the woman. He would be killed before he ever reached that weapon. The barn, though, that was filled with tools, some of them very sharp. He might be able to fend them off. Hurt one, maybe. Louis stood, being careful to make no noise, doing nothing that would attract their attention. But none of that mattered.

The donkey stared through the window at Louis. Then, the beast lowered its head and made a sound, like two voices screaming in harmony. A hatchet, its blade dug in past the bit, stuck out between the animal's shoulders.

What had Thomas said, that morning?

Sunk it deep in the withers.

Louis knew there was nothing he could do except watch the horror unfold, and even that would be short-lived.

The donkey turned its attention to Hattie. It pulled at the torn hem of her dress, rooting under the skirt until its whole head burrowed beneath and pushed towards her sex. The material at the crotch darkened as the beast tugged violently on unseen flesh. Hattie's screams were so much like Elliot's own pathetic howls, as if those notes were a song to be sung, as if being eating alive was just another ritual.

James had once confided to Louis that screams are a hymnal every creature can sing. Pain is proselytizing. Death is the one, true faith. And everyone worships in their due time.

Louis stumbled backwards. The corner of the dining table bit him in the thigh and he fell to the ground. His head cracked against the wooden floor, but when he passed out it was not from the blow. Sheer terror exhausted him and sleep took him.

He dreamed of Ruth and Danny.

Sleep held strong for several hours, but Louis finally opened his eyes. The sun hung low on the horizon and shadows cut darkly at severe angles. He remained still and listened. A breeze outside whipped by, not in fits and starts but as a steady current, sounding not unlike a gentle stream, the occasional scattering of dry soil and brush the only betrayal of that illusion. He tried to imagine himself as a child by the creek near the old family farm, one of the few places he ever felt at peace. But peace, then, had only been temporary, an illusion. The past and the present were no different.

He rolled to his side and pushed up off the floor.

The feral asses were gone. Hattie was gone, too. Most of her, anyway.

Louis gathered himself at the back door, bracing for what he'd see and smell. His only frame of reference for this kind of carnage had been helping his father clean game hen and the occasional hog, and the only dead body he ever saw sat in a coffin at a church. These meager experiences were ill preparation, he knew, but he stepped outside because he wanted the shotgun. It would soon be dark. They would return.

All that remained of Hattie was a single foot and a wad of hair still attached to scalp. Her dress lay about in pieces, the largest of which had been picked up by the breeze and tangled in the jagged, ruined fence. The ground had been stained an unnatural shade and it glistened in the waning light, smelling sickly sweet. Flies swarmed, rising and falling like a buzzing black tide, their movement and hum hypnotic. Louis found himself being pulled into a sea of blood.

His foot sank in a soft spot of dark earth and what had been Hattie seeped out of the ground. That crimson whisper broke the fly's spell and Louis retreated backwards. Only then did he realize he'd been holding his breath. He sucked in through his teeth and tasted her ruin. The smell was nauseating.

The gun, Louis reminded himself. The double-barrel had been no more than a few feet away, but no longer. Had the animals kicked it away? And then he found it.

Like Hattie, the shotgun had been destroyed and existed in scattered pieces. The stock shattered from the butt to the trigger guard. Forestock busted in half, the ass end still clinging to the barrel, itself bent just an inch or so from the muzzle and front sight. Bastards stomped it to Hell.

They knew, Louis thought. They were only goddamned animals but they knew all the same.

Perhaps, he thought, the beasts were like his brother James. Born from pain and nursed on violence. Maybe what they were on the inside didn't match up with how they looked on the outside.

Thomas had said that he recognized what the animals looked like but he didn't know what they were, and Louis understood that implicitly. After all, he barely thought of James as human. It stood to reason that Louis had been wrong to think of these donkeys as mere animals. He realized that, now.

Oh, God . . . *Thomas.*

The patriarch would be back soon. Louis tried to think of what to tell him, but he knew that nothing would suffice. The scene behind the home would tell Thomas all he needed to know, except—

Matthias.

Louis ran inside. He called out but got no answer. The house had but three rooms. There was nowhere to hide in the main room, an open space that stretched from the front of the home to the back. The kitchen cabinets were high off of the floor and much too small for the boy, and he wasn't under the table. Louis looked up inside the fireplace but the chimney flue was likewise too small for a boy his size. Both bedrooms lined the east side. The smaller room belonged to Matthias. He was neither curled up beneath the bed nor crouched in the small wardrobe. The door to Thomas and Hattie's room was locked. Louis knocked.

"Matthias," Louis said. "Open the door."

No movement from inside the room and no sound, save the roving winds outside.

Louis pressed his shoulder into the door, but the lock held strong. He stepped back and kicked the door. The frame cracked loudly and Louis could feel the lock give. He kicked it a second time, then a third and final. The door swung open, the screws holding the lock in place taking a considerable bite out of the frame. Like the smaller room, there was only a bed and a wardrobe, though both were much bigger. But Matthias seemed to have vanished. Louis sat on the foot of the bed and listening to the breeze, feeling the air. He turned around.

The window had been pulled open. Not all the way, Matthias wouldn't have needed to open it all the way to slip through. Louis stuck his head out.

A straight shot, once you hit the ground, from that window to the barn. The loft in there would make a pretty good hiding place, too. Louis went outside.

Louis couldn't tell from inside the house, but the barn door had been opened enough for someone to slip inside. He called the boy's name but got the same nothing as inside the house. He climbed the ladder to the loft. No Matthias.

The loft stretched the entire length of the barn's north side, and Louis paced back and forth. He stopped in his tracks, looking over the edge of the loft towards the floor. The well seemed an unlikely place for the boy to hide, but it remained the only spot Louis hadn't checked.

Louis heaved the large, wooden cap off the top of the well. He looked inside but the cavity was impossibly dark. He would need more light. A brass and copper oil lamp hung from a hook by the barn door, but he would need matches or a lighter or, at the very least, a flint.

That he quit smoking years ago now flooded him with a

strange remorse.

He trotted back to the house and made his way to the kitchen. The cupboards contained nothing of use. A quick rummage through the pantry proved far more fruitful.

The Ronson lighter was a polished silver. Both sides were pinstriped but only one side had a smooth oval at the center. *To Thomas*—in cursive—had been engraved in the oval. Louis shook the lighter and felt the fluid move inside. He pressed the button and the lighter sparked and the wick lit. Louis sighed.

"Thank God."

Louis returned to the barn but stopped at the door. He craned his neck and turned an ear upward. Sounded like a hawk in the distance. But he knew it to be no hawk.

Louis walked to the south corner of the barn. A hint of movement in the distance caught his attention. The cart's wheels sounding less like birdsong and more like the shrill grind of metal on metal.

How long, thought Louis? Ten minutes, maybe twenty. Would Thomas find fault with what Hattie had considered the natural order? Louis feared becoming a target for the man's grief. Louis thought to arm himself. He retreated to the barn, leaving the door wide open.

The scythe weighed more than Louis anticipated. The curved handle had been fashioned from dense wood. The blade had been kept sharp. Evening sun pushed in on Louis like a spotlight.

The clopping of horse hooves now joined the squeal of the cart. The wooden frame of the vehicle jostled in a rickety fashion. Louis dripped sweat. The horse stepped into view and Louis tightened his grip on the scythe. His stomach sank.

The horse and the cart were covered in dried blood. A single handprint stained the grain along the side of the cart. The horse paid Louis no mind, only tried to drag itself into its stable. The cart's width made that impossible, so the horse simply stood there, as if waiting to be released from the vehicle. Louis stepped outside to look around.

No sign of Thomas anywhere. Something much more alarming, however, sat to the west. The sun turned deepest orange, like burning paper, and the horizon glowed with a redness that bled up and into the darkening sky. Louis ran back into the barn, hoping there would be enough wood to start any kind of bonfire before night fell completely.

He looked into the cart but reflex caused him to turn and gag. The animals had left more of Hattie than Thomas, but what they had left sent a message, loud and clear. Louis wondered if the piece of flesh in the back of the cart had been plucked from Thomas while he lived. Louis wanted to believe the man did not experience his own castration. That gnawed, pitiful flesh represented his future were they to catch him.

He needed fire and he needed it fast.

Louis gathered the few pieces of wood that Thomas managed to load, which consisted of an armful and nothing more. Not nearly enough for the type of fire that had burned the previous night. Louis ran to the back of the house and picked up the broken pieces of fence, hardly any more than kindling, really. Desperation set in until Louis realized there was so much more inside the house. After all, no one was coming home.

He could burn it all if he wanted.

Louis pulled out their beds, first. Then, he dragged their wardrobes to the pile. The kitchen table, next, and the four chairs, carried individually and heaped onto the rest. The last of the ritual, however, remained a mystery. Did Thomas light the fire while light yet shimmered on the horizon, or would he wait until the desert sank into one endless shadow? The ritual belonged to Louis, now, and he would do what felt right. He saw no reason to wait until dark.

He wrapped a bit of torn, oil-spattered bedsheet around the end of a splintered bit of fence and then lit that on fire. Louis felt a moment of pride as his homemade torch burned brightly. He circled the pile, lighting small fires along the base as he went. After a few minutes, the bonfire roared and spat a pillar of black smoke into the sky. He hoped it would be enough.

The sun dipped well below the distant horizon and the sky in the west colored like a deep and painful bruise. Black sky stretched from the east. In a matter of minutes, even the bruised horizon disappeared. Not a star in the heavens. The whole universe conspired against Louis, he could feel it. He would've been stricken blind if not for the fire. The sky, in all its enormity, held nothing of awe or wonder to him in that moment.

Louis did not believe in God. That didn't stop him from cursing Him under his breath.

I'll show you, he thought. And he marched into the home.

Louis stood in that very living room, hours earlier, with a man and woman and their child. All that remained of the family now hung from a nail in the wall. Their guardian angel had abandoned them to the *natural order*. Louis shook with anger and spoke through gritted teeth.

"You don't even deserve the cross they nailed you to."

He threw the lamp and screamed. Glass shattered. Fire bloomed. The cross on the wall turned black, folding in on itself like a wilting flower. Flames spread across the front of the home and crept along the floorboards to the bedrooms. Smoke thickened until the inside became a glowing fog. Toxic fumes billowed out the front door and through broken windows.

Louis retreated to the barn and climbed to the loft. The burning home threw wild light like sharpened claws. Shadows danced about and dark waves which pummeled the fire threatened to drown the light, treating illumination as if it were an abomination to be snuffed out.

He would saddle the horse in the morning and ride to Adel. He would—

"Mommy."

Louis couldn't be sure he heard a voice. The fire raged, outside, crackling and consuming, pouring up into the night. If he pressed himself to the wall then he could see between the boards, little slivers of the world outside his hiding place.

Louis had searched for the boy but never dreamed of looking on the roof.

Matthias ran back and forth in a panic, wailing for his mother. A loud cracking preceded the opening of the hole which swallowed Matthias, dropping the boy down into the burning home. His screams were worse than Elliot's or Hattie's, more pathetic, with a silly quality, like children sound when they chase each other till they're out of breath. Those notes the boy hit had the quality of innocence extinguished.

Louis gasped when Matthias spilled into the yard, his hair and back on fire.

"I'm coming," Louis said, but he froze.

The four of them raced out of the darkness and set upon Matthias.

Louis turned away, tears streaming. He sat with his back

against the wall, pressed his hands to his ears, and rocked back and forth. Every scream chilled him to the bone, to the marrow. It was no longer enough to simply not see what was happening, because hearing and imagining became somehow worse, so Louis screamed, too.

Their hymnal could be heard for miles around, by every creature in the dark.

Louis screamed his throat raw, his mouth tasted of blood, but he kept screaming, and did so for a very long time. But by now he screamed alone. The ritual ended long ago, and the four beasts returned to the darkness, each carrying within them some part of the family who had invaded their land.

The house yet burned at first light.

Louis peered through the boards for a stretch, sometimes moving to a different bit of sliver, so as to get a better view. Once satisfied that nothing waited for him, outside, he willed himself down from the loft. He stopped just inside the entrance to the barn and looked to the ground. The donkeys left a bit of bloodied, uncircumcised flesh for Louis to find.

He could no longer cry, even if he wanted to. No voice left with which to call out, to curse. Whatever strength remained he would need for the long ride ahead.

The horse remained at the entrance to the stable. Louis knew he would have to lose the cart. The extra weight would slow the animal down. He could not take that chance. Adel before darkness, anything less than that meant death.

Undoing the hitch took less time than he imagined, and after several minutes he rolled the cart away. All he needed to do was swap the cart saddle for the riding saddle. Taking off the cart saddle proved easy, but when it came time to put on the riding saddle, the horse became agitated. Louis stroked the horse's neck, like Thomas had done, but the animal reared.

"Shit!"

The power and size of the animal startled him. Louis scrambled backwards. The back of his knees hit the edge of the well and he completely lost balance.

As he fell headfirst into the darkness, Louis thought about Ruth and Danny and he wondered if their screams would sound anything like Elliot's. No one would save them from James.

And then, Louis slammed into the water with enough force to wind him. His lungs filled as he sank into the earth. Louis became a corpse almost immediately.

The well became a grave.

PART TWO

Angels of the trees, those delicate raptors with their hollow bones, they took their birdsong and flew south to Hell, leaving the green church silent. Red and yellow and orange laid waste to the trees in the valley below, an autumnal blaze amongst the nave. Higher in the Oregon mountains, pines in the crossing remained evergreen and refused to die. The man who wandered those woods thought himself a sanctuary, his mouth a censer, and his breath prayer. Both hands acted as a single altar. Sermon like a serpent coiled within him, a great and twisted pain which readied its strike and sat heavy on the heart. No mere hymn would suffice for his parishioners. He had heard enough of their hymns.

An engine roared in the distance. Tires spun out on dirt and gravel, commanded by one who must've been unfamiliar with the path, a stranger to this holy temple, a heathen. Rare were the days when one chose to enter the emerald tabernacle. Even the parishioners who were chosen often acted out in fear. To be saved, to give of one's self and receive salvation, proved no easy task. How many had fought his wisdom and word? How many came to the altar, untamed and afraid? Wayward souls often displayed these weaknesses before they could be given release.

However, he had never failed anyone before, and he would not fail whoever approached at this early hour. Did this person know that they were driving towards their own salvation? Would they beg? Would they deny their own ransom? Surely they would, as all the rest had done. This fact did not matter.

A car appeared, followed by the billowing smoke of disturbed dirt as if the vision had been yawned into existence by ancient earth. The side of the car was painted with large, black letters: State Police. The automobile rolled to a stop at quite a distance. Many, many years had passed since the last time one of these men was reformed. But all parishioners were roughly the same and easily disarmed.

The sanctuary kept both altars at his sides and offered a smile, as warm and as welcoming as you'd give a long-lost relative. He could wear a smile like that for days. And then James waved.

The parishioner approached the sanctuary. He kept his hat on, but parishioners like this often felt that they were above the rituals of the church. However, he had at least the decency to tip the brim as salutation, so his demeanor wasn't one of total ignorance.

"Are you James Hayte?" the parishioner asked.

James nodded in affirmation.

"You got a brother named Louis Hayte? Goes by the alias Louis Loving?"

Louis . . . that name struck like lightning to a hollow oak and something inside the sanctuary split in two, smoldered and burned. The sermon took shape like dark clouds at a distant horizon, words like a cool wind promising a baptismal rain. And that name, which hadn't been heard or spoken in many years, lit a blasphemous fire which welcomed the coming maelstrom. All the while, James smiled and nodded.

"Have you seen or had any contact with your brother at any time within the last three weeks?"

"Louis stole my Ruth."

"He's wanted in connection to some murders."

"I'm the one he done wrong, you hear?"

The sanctuary lunged forward and the parishioner fought, as expected. But it became clear that strength and rage were on the side of James and the parishioner tried to flee. He kicked and crawled and screamed for the sake of screaming. No one would hear him. After all, the angels of the trees had gone. Heathen he may be, yet he knew the hymns that preceded deliverance. His voice was lovely and high-pitched, a good tenor.

James wrapped an arm around the man's neck and the man became limp. The parishioner snored almost as loudly as he had screamed. James chuckled and smiled at the sound.

The parishioner awoke on the dirt floor of the sacristy, a wooden shed at the back of the property. Instinct drew his hand to his holster, but it was empty. The revolver pointed at him, from across the sacristy, held at the end of the altar.

"You know where my brother is," James said. "So I figure you know where Ruth is, too."

"He went missing. I told you."

"Yeah, you sure did. Said him's a murderer."

"I never said that."

"You got two eyes and I can see inside you. Now, you came here, yeah? You go anywhere else? You go see my Ruth?"

"He went missing near a small farm outside Adel. That's all I know, mister."

"Did you know a dead body is the end of a prayer? That the only amen is oblivion?"

"Jesus . . . Jesus Christ, mister."

"Damned are the poor in spirit, you know." James reached

into his pants pocket and pulled out a picture. "While you were resting I poked around your britches and found a photo of a sweet-looking kid. Bet that sweetness is waiting at the address I saw on your license."

The parishioner begged and pleaded, just as all who came to the altar begged and pleaded, singing a variation of the tune known to so many others. He loved God and Jesus and he would go and live his days free of sin and how he would be a good man. He sang about his wife, for a time, but most of his song praised the child. Pure as the driven snow, he sang, pure as a lily. Then, he offered charities. The parishioner dumped loose change and paper monies all about the floor. He turned his pockets inside out to show that he had no more to give.

James leaned forward. "Of course you have more."

The parishioner smiled, attempted at any rate, and laughed a silly laugh but also cried some. He took off his gold wedding band and practically threw it to the altar. And then he took off his watch and held it out, that weak and stupid smile still tethered to his sweaty face. His head bobbed up and down, as though these material things were any substitute for flesh and blood.

"You have more to give."

That stupid smile disappeared. Lips quivered, now, and the parishioner blubbered and shook. He offered his shoes, his shirt, and pants.

"You go out as you came in."

What a face he made, then, that wet and wrinkled frown. He took off his underwear and stood before the sanctuary, as naked as any newborn child, but fearful and embarrassed. He cupped both hands over his genitals.

"You go on and turn around, now, and lay on the floor."

James took off his clothes.

What the altar received next wasn't exactly given, but the revolver said it wanted to watch, and hardly anybody said no to a revolver. James and that gun took the man for a ride around the dirt floor until the air heated like a summer day. Clouds of dust kicked up, an earthy steam, like the ground worked as hard as they. The parishioner cried out in ecstasy and shame, and then the altar whispered in his ear.

"Would you like to die, now?"

"Yes." He cried and put a hand over his eyes. "Please, God, yes."

"It pleases God." The sanctuary stood above him. "I promise."

Brains leaked out the parishioner's ears by the time James left him and he would never be any deader. You could not tell what had been blood or sweat or seed. All of it was dirt, now.

James Hayte walked from the sacristy across the west transept and into the dilapidated barn. He grabbed two cans of petrol. The first can he emptied along the inside of the barn. Before he left, he nodded in the direction of a skeletal cadaver that hung from a rope tied to the highest ceiling beams. "Goodbye," he said. What remained of the petrol was taken to the shed and poured over the body and the doorway. He emptied the second can inside his childhood home. One match for each structure was all it took.

Smoke leached through the wood siding and rolled out of windows, a lazy nightmare that poured into the sky like a black waterfall in reverse. Dark fingers crept up and around the tree branches, climbed higher and higher until they choked the sky. The burning home cast a light deep into the church, in every direction, and stole away the shadow and shade. But memories burned brighter.

Flames burst forth and grew in intensity, becoming a living light, like a circle, like an eye, which swathed all in effulgence so bright that James saw nothing else. No other light as pure, this light like a river, which issued sparks and issued embers, and they were like rubies floating in gold. Impossibly, the river swelled, devoured leaf and tree above and, in its great thirst, took even the dirt below. Destruction as miracle, destruction as a birth, what had been simply a home revealed itself to be Empyrean.

Heaven.

A single ember shone deeper than the rest, like a crimson star in the blinding distance, and it held James's attention. It sizzled and turned the color of coal. Dark wings revealed themselves from within the blazing circumference and the phantasm flew through the portal, abandoned the perfect chaos of Providence for the crippled reality of creation.

James followed the harbinger away from the pure light and walked down into the great nave where the brilliance of the fire flickered and teased shape and form and dancing figures. He kept those cavorting imps to his periphery and refused to look away from the misshapen gloom whose wings beat fiercely. What was it becoming?

James froze and the hair on his neck stood.

He felt as though he were being watched. He let the sensation steal his attention and he peered ahead. What he saw caused him to laugh and shake his head. He wiped his eyes and looked a second time.

A lamb and a dog and a dove blocked the path.

James smiled at the vision before him and took a step towards the animals.

The dog's lips folded back like a tide. You couldn't count the beast's teeth if you wanted. Each one bled at the root and each one moved. A mouthful of ivory shards. The lamb screamed and the dove fluttered its wings hard enough that feathers fell like snow in a blizzard. The three of them meant to be his keeper.

A shrill whistle rained down from above, a noise that could only have come from a beast of hollow bones. Yet, this note was not quite birdsong. James craned his neck.

The emissary from Empyrean had composed itself as a stately raven, an ebony bird whose ashen skull held no flesh, whose eyes were fiery, ominous globes. It perched upon a busted palace branch.

"Tell me what your name is, ghastly raven."

Said the raven, *"Josh Billings being duly sworn, testifys az follers: yu kan kount on Josh Billings az a frend."*

"Billings." James wondered aloud. "Name means nothing to me, grim and ungainly bird."

The raven swooped down from busted branch and all that followed next happened in the space of a few breaths.

Billings attacked the three animals. The angered hound snapped and growled. Billings squawked, flapped its wings in the dog's face, then flew up and out of reach. The dog leaped after, and Billings stretched out both sets of claws and plucked out the dog's eyes.

While the dog still fell, Billings dipped low and flung those bloodied globes into the throat of the screaming lamb. The woolen animal choked and slumped to its side. It convulsed as it gagged. The lamb's eyes rolled up into its head as it died.

The dog hit the ground and scratched and clawed the earth and snapped in all directions. Poor dove wandered too close. Those shifting, innumerable canine teeth cleaved dove's little body clean in two. Feathers ceased to fall, like a waning storm. The dog's body shuddered and the beast relieved itself, while lungs sighed for a final time, a melancholy howl before entering a night that never ends.

And the path through the nave opened once more.

James looked to the raven, Billings, who hopped from one dead animal to the next and ate what tender and raw bits had been exposed in the scuffle.

"Why have you done this?" James asked.

Billings ceased his carrion comforts and faced James.

"In olden times the brokers and dove pedlars were hustled out ov the temple ov God, and it would be medicine tew me to see this great temple, made without hands, cleaned ov the two dollar and fifty cent vermin that infest it."

"You mean for me to take my sermon beyond the nave and straight to the congregation."

"Yu kant konvert sinners bi preaching the gospel tew them at haff price."

Billings spread his wings and flew to James, and then came to rest on the man's right shoulder. Claws sank into flesh, but the wounds soothed James. He found Billings to have a cheerful countenance, which comforted him as they went into the secret things beyond the green church.

Neither man nor bird looked behind them to the growing fire. The church hummed with the bright light of consuming heaven. Destruction crackled and sizzled and belched up the black soot of creation. Sanctuary uprooted itself with purpose. Sermon demanded deliverance. For too many years, James had been content to spread the word of Almighty Death only to those who wandered into the church. No longer. He would take the good news to the heathens and bless them with final repose.

Homicide for the reluctant. Suicide for the willing. All were victim to nascicide, regardless, delivered from a coffin called mother and father, death begetting death, forever and ever, since time immemorial. Only through the sermon could they be made wise, could they understand. They would know their future.

Oblivion.

The sun set as James and Billings approached the narthex. There the green church ended and the only trees thereafter were scattered in the occasional copse. Here on were the paved roads, the black veins of community, which ran between homes, further, to the engorged towns and larger cities whose false stars polluted the wash of darkness gifted by setting sun. False light for false prophets and heathens, an artificial heaven filled with lies.

Billings squawked. *"Human knowledge is very short, and don't reach but a little ways, and even that little ways iz twilite."*

James pulled out the picture of the child. Not pictured, a mother, whom James knew to exist, though he possessed no photo of her. After all, the parishioner had sung a song about her not an hour prior. James fished the parishioner's license from his back pocket.

"Damned are those who mourn the dead, for life cannot comfort them. Only in death is a true comfort rewarded." James held the license up for Billings to see. "Can you take me to this address?"

Billings cocked his skeletal head and focused a fiery eye—which floated in its black hollow socket—until it was a red star no larger than the head of a pin yet as bright as a beam from atop a lighthouse. He scanned the parishioner's address, cawed, and then took to the air.

"There are only formless things in this void, Billings." Then James said, "I need to see."

Light from the bird's eyes divided the darkness ahead and James followed.

In a modest, one-story home at the edge of town, Marylou examined the clock on the wall in the kitchen. She wondered about her husband, Henry, and wondered when he would finally come home. The man was rarely ever late. His dinner had waited on the table for over an hour until she finally moved it to the oven. His evening paper she placed on the couch, his pipe and glass of brandy on the coffee table. He would expect her to wait up for him, so that is what she did. Their daughter, Alice, slept in her room at the other side of the house, unaware of her mother's concerns, blissfully so, as her mother intended. What passed for a neighborhood on the outskirts of town was voiceless, save the occasional hoot of a faraway owl and dim lights of other homes in the distance.

She tiptoed down the hallway and looked in on the sleeping child. Alice had kicked off her covers and her bangs dampened darkly and stuck to her skin. The temperature on this side of the house was always higher than the rest. Marylou cracked open a window to let in some of the cool night air and give a spot of relief to the poor girl. She tucked her daughter in and shut the bedroom door as lightly as possible.

Marylou jumped when she heard the knock at her front door.

A knock, a ring of the telephone, both sounds a constant source of dread for the wife of a policeman, especially one who had promised to be home in time for dinner. She felt a deep fear that quickened her heart and caused her to chew her fingernails to nubs. And this knock—no, pounding—on the door at this hour presented so many fears simultaneously.

Henry may have had an accident, like a car crash or an arrest gone awry. Could be that he had died, or even worse, it could be Henry came home drunk and ready to pour all of his dumb anger into her. And she would let him, no matter how many times, no matter how badly it hurt, she would let him. At least until Alice was old enough to get away.

Or it could be that the cops finally put two and two together and figured out that he was a no-good sonofabitch. Maybe he'd gone to jail for shaking down a citizen. Marylou had often expected that Henry would end up ruining her life.

There was no way any of this was going to end well. Fear was becoming the norm. Marylou wanted a way out.

"Who is it?" she asked.

"Ma'am, there's been an accident. Can you help me locate my Ruth, by any chance?"

"My husband works for the state police."

"Oh, I know all about that. I already talked to him, see, but I wanted to do a little follow-up with you, if you don't mind. Maybe you can put my mind at ease."

"I'm sorry, mister, but I'm"—she hesitated to come up with an excuse—"getting ready for work. And I can't be late. You can come back tomorrow and talk to my husband."

He didn't answer right away. Only the faintest rhythmic sounds, as if he were drumming his fingers on the other side of the door. Marylou smelled something foul, unwashed skin and male musk, but something else, too, like burnt wood. There was a heavy sigh, very dramatic, very put upon. And then it got quiet for a moment.

"Now I know for a fact—*a fact*—that you don't go into work at night. I'll even wager that you're in there wearing a nightgown and getting ready to worry yourself to sleep about that husband of yours. Bet you done put that sweet child to bed, too. You let me know if that sounds clear as a bell."

He was right, of course, but she didn't want to humor him.

"Mister, I'd really appreciate it if we could do this tomorrow."

"I'd really appreciate it if we could do this right now. Don't make me ask again."

"You can't threaten me. I know my rights."

"You never had a right in your life."

"This is really starting to aggravate me, now, mister. I'd like you to leave or I'll report you for harassment. I'll call the police."

James liked the way she said *poh-leeze*.

"Go on, then." He laughed. "I'll tell you what, if you can get them on the phone I'll go lay down in the yard, here, and wait for them to show up. Scout's honor."

Marylou darted from the door and into the kitchen where Henry had mounted their rotary phone to the wall. She grabbed the handset and spun the chrome dial, but only once. Silence greeted her when she placed the handset to her ear. She punched the switch hook a couple times in desperation. The line was dead.

Suddenly there came a tapping, a gentle rapping, from the front door. Marylou knew to grab a knife, a tactic which helped subdue her husband in the past. And then the visitor whispered his intentions, whispered so that hearing was a chore. Marylou pressed an ear against the entry.

"You're as safe as a rat in a trap. Better to open up and talk. Tell me what you know about Ruth and I'll be on my way."

"I don't know nothing about no Ruth, mister. Now, please, leave."

"You know, the only people that ever put up this much of a fight are the ones with something to hide. Is that what you want me to think, ma'am, that you're hiding something?"

"I'm hiding from a crazy person, is all."

"You're a lot smarter than your husband, I'll give you that. You know he came to me and didn't even have the sense to draw a weapon? You should know his last words were about you. And your child."

A chill ran through her arms and legs. She had no response to his implication, no cutting remark. She had always believed news of Henry's death would come as a relief. She backed away from the door and trembled.

"Who are you?"

"I am a sanctuary for the truth which saved that husband of yours, saved a whole mess of people. I intend to save you and your daughter, too, whether you want it or not, but first you have to talk to me, Marylou. We can turn this around. You and me, make it right."

"You're insane."

"Depends on your definition, I suppose. I may just be the sanest man you'll ever meet. Right now, all over the world, there's a lot of people's lives all busted up because of a great deceiver. Yours included, am I right? He says believe in him and you'll live forever. Well, I'm telling you that forever is damnation. Salvation is only capable through acquiescence to silent oblivion. The deceiver, though, he holds oblivion ransom and tells you to live your life till it runs its course. That is a prison sentence, Marylou. Imagine stepping into Hell and staying there of your own volition. That . . . is insanity. But it doesn't have to be. Not if you help me."

"When Henry doesn't report in to the station they'll come looking for him. Police are probably on their way."

"Eventually they'll come knocking. Right now, I imagine

they're busy tending to the fire. Your husband, he said a name to me which I haven't heard in a very long time. Maybe if I run it by you, then you can tell me what you know, and then we can get this over with."

Marylou steadied herself and trembles gave way to resolve. She reached out for the door knob, but hesitated. Her grip on the knife's handle caused blood to drain from the joints, as if the closed fist burned white hot. If the visitor wanted a confrontation, then a confrontation she would give him. However strong the man might think himself, his strength didn't equal that of a sharpened steel blade. She looked askance to the cross which hung above the fireplace and her spirit became a stone slab. She hesitated no longer and swung wide the door.

Marylou lunged at nothing more than darkness. No madman stood outside the entry door, only night and the call of the distant owl greeted her. But then she noticed something more.

A huge, obsidian bird—whose head held neither feather nor skin, whose eyes glowed like dying embers—outstretched both wings and opened wide its skeletal mouth and spoke.

"Every body luvs tew phool with the chances, bekauze every body expects tew win. But I am authorized tew state that every body don't win."

Marylou screamed. The stone slab inside her crumbled at this vision. She retreated within her home, slammed the door, and held the knife before her.

She peered at the door, and in her mind, she gazed well beyond the door into the vast darkness. She wondered and she feared, wanted so badly to doubt, and yet she could not will herself from this waking dream.

And then, once more, she thought she heard a whisper, and thinking that her visitor returned, she placed an ear against the door. But no whisper waited, yet an echo sounded of that whisper heard before. And the air, it chilled, and moved around her, set to agitate her, a ghostly embrace meant to carry her away, or catch her attention. She could not be certain, but thought it best to back away from that door.

Then she realized that the whisper she thought she heard and the draft which caressed her bare skin were one and the same. Had the temperature in the house not dropped since his arrival? Had she not opened the window in which this draft found purchase? She walked across the living room but ran down the hallway. She screamed her daughter's name and, to her horror, the door she'd closed stood open, now. What had been a draft and a whisper revealed itself to be the cold night pouring in through a window thrown wide open, a cavernous maw, a black well that stretched to infinity. She felt blindly for the switch and turned the light on and she braced herself against the horror she thought she'd find.

Alice sat up in bed, unharmed. Dread left Marylou and her arms and legs flooded with a warm relief. She allowed herself to laugh. Awake, after all, she thought to herself. Alice smiled at the sound, rubbed her eyes, and then pointed towards her mother.

"Mommy, who's that man?"

Marylou felt the blow to the back of her head but lost consciousness before hitting the floor. That didn't stop her from being chilled by night air or hearing Alice scream in terror.

Marylou traded one horrible dream for another. She ran through an impenetrable darkness. Her daughter's screams bellowed from every direction. Marylou tried to call out to Alice but her mouth refused to work. All she could manage were pitiful moans.

Then, again, his whisper, which cut through her stupor and

sunk into her like a hook, dragged her up and out of the black depths, one horrible dream for another.

Marylou woke up tied to a chair. She thought her attacker sat across from her, but as her vision focused she saw that Alice, likewise, had been tied to a chair, bound and gagged. The child's eyes were wide and her tears flowed free, soaking the cloth used to silence her. Marylou looked down. The knife she had grabbed from the kitchen sat in her lap. She stretched out her fingers and the tight bindings cut into her skin. Five inches, maybe, but those inches may as well have been miles. She blubbered for a moment and mouthed "I'm sorry" to her daughter.

Though he stayed out of sight, Marylou knew the man had to be close by. The smell of his dirty flesh overwhelmed her. She blinked away tears.

Breath tickled the back of Marylou's neck. His words sent a shock through her body.

"Earth is an eye and we are the detached retina. This globe spins wildly in its black socket, sees little more than tricks of light, reflections of color. We look on in terror, always terror. Love is terror. I think you know that, now."

"Please don't hurt Alice." She sobbed. "Please don't hurt my little lamb."

Marylou craned her neck to try and see him, but the binds were simply too tight. The man stood at her periphery, shapeless, poorly defined. A loud caw like a wretched laugh announced itself from behind her. The awful thing she'd seen outside spoke, somewhere at the back of the living room, though she guessed it perched near the fireplace.

"When a lam gits thru being a lam, they immejiately bekum a sheep. This takes all the sentiment out ov them. There ain't mutch poetry in mutton."

"Quiet, Billings," he said. "I'll handle this."

The man walked around her chair, his footsteps silent, as if he had no weight to him at all, and he presented himself to Marylou. His pallor suggested a vagabond ghost, a dirty corpse reanimated, a visage which complemented the malodorous fragrance that preceded him.

Marylou said, "You don't have to hurt my baby, mister. Whatever you want, this ain't worth it."

James kneeled in front of Marylou. He placed a hand on her knee. Her trembles echoed through his arm. He smiled up at the woman and patted her thigh.

"I'd be lying if I said this was all from the bottom of my heart," James said, and then stood up. "I definitely have a dog in this race, but that's between me and my Ruth."

"I'll tell you whatever you want if you promise to let my little girl go."

He seemed to weigh her request in his mind, his pondering expressed by the way he screwed up his mouth. His eyes wandered the room. Brow furrowed in disappointment and he nodded his head, like he expected the letdown. He marched across the room, out of sight, but returned quickly and swapped the knife in Marylou's lap for the cross that had hung above the fireplace.

James pointed the butcher knife at Marylou.

"If you had to pick one person, who would you say that your husband confides in the most? Who's his best friend, his drinking buddy? Who do you think is special enough to be privy to Henry's little adventures?"

"Oh. That's easy. His name's Alton." She smiled. "They work together, drinking buddies, like you said, they're always laughing. Inside jokes, that's what they call it."

"Inside jokes," he said. He looked to the floor and shook his head. "Is that what they think of my Ruth?"

"My Alice is a good girl, mister. Pure as a lily. She loves Jesus. She takes communion every Sunday." Marylou thought of all the time spent in the pews. They were the only hours of the week Henry afforded her to be on her lonesome. She hated that church.

"Every Sunday," Marylou whispered.

"Only the damned consume each other. Their communion is unending, eating one another, living and thriving on death just to stretch out torment. Of course you need to believe in lies. You live in Hell. That's what the deceiver offers you. Flesh of his flesh, blood of his blood, all that, it's nothing more than the sick joke of a cannibal. Greville said we are created sick, commanded to be sound, but he was wrong. We are only ever commanded to die, and the sooner the better. Living long is sacrilege. Even God wants to die. And we are made in His image."

"There's nothing of God in you."

The man glared at Marylou, obviously struck silent by her admonition. His sudden taciturnity alarmed the woman, as he seemed to be ordering his thoughts, making decisions, and his expressions shifted, as if he were engaged in a frantic inner dialogue. But then he stood very still, very poised, and he held the knife before him as if he listened to the blade's secrets. He looked towards Alice and then smiled at Marylou.

"Do you want to see who God favors?" James pointed the blade at Marylou. "Ask Him to save you."

She stammered a poor request for divine intervention. James held a hand to his ear as if straining to listen. He looked up to the ceiling and then back to Marylou. He shook his head.

"No, nothing? Now"—James raised the knife—"I shall ask

Him to guide this blade into your child's heart."

He crossed between mother and daughter and stood in front of Alice. Marylou couldn't see what was happening, but then James stepped aside. She wished to see no more.

"See?" James asked. "It is I to whom God listens."

The bloodied child, bound, and without use of her mouth, elected to scream with her eyes. And then James blocked Marylou's view once more. Though she couldn't see what he was doing, Marylou shut her eyes. Hearing him work was bad enough and the sounds made her ill.

"Wonder whare all the happiness on earth goes to when it dies." Billings squawked.

Something heavy, but soft, and warm, fell into her lap. Her nightgown soaked through and what she could not bring herself to look upon dripped onto the floor, ran in rivulets between her legs, and pooled in the chair. Pungent sweetness cut through the man's odor.

James leaned close to her. "Would you like to die, now?"

"Yes." Marylou cried.

She would never open her eyes again.

Mother and daughter were soon indistinguishable from one another, and when James left their modest home they would never be any deader. Billings, again, blazed through the ink of nighttime by way of his bright eyes. Through this crimson lens, James could see the stars above.

Then James said, "The heavens appear raw, like a fresh scab on an old wound."

Across town, Henry's friend, Alton, startled awake.

Alton had another nightmare, though this one saw the townsfolk become a mob who forced him to kill his wife and child before turning the gun on himself. He woke up before committing to his end. Bed sheets moistened with his sweat and cooled against his skin. His wife breathed heavily and sounded far away, but before he could wake her a rank odor announced itself. Alton smelled his own armpit. He leaned across to smell his wife. Perhaps something crawled beneath the house and died?

The bedroom was a dark and hot womb. Curtains were pulled closed, the blinds drawn. There was, on occasion, the sound of a truck on the nearby highway. That rush of tread across asphalt, the bark of hungry engines, punctuated by the rhythmic current of an early morning breeze which cut through the basin valley like exasperation.

The air outside whispered to Alton. A steady tempest worked itself into a shrill lament outside the bedroom window, as if a pained and restless spirit begged for a house to haunt. Alton wanted nothing to do with ghosts. He put his hand out and felt his wife next to him, her sleep went undisturbed. Her body felt cool so he pulled the covers to her shoulders.

The electric clock on her side of the bed constituted the lone source of dim light. He wiped his eyes. The time read 3:30, what his yaya called *tiempo muerto*. Dead time. The witching hour.

A shadow had come to life and stood at the end of the bed. Alton spied its outline in the darkness. He thought his mind played tricks, but the shadow spoke and Alton froze.

"Don't make a sound," James said, not quite a whisper. "Do you understand? I found the gun you keep on your nightstand. I have it pointed at your head."

"Please don't hurt my family."

"Get up. Go to your living room. You and I are going to have words."

Alton's eyes had adjusted enough that he made his way with relative ease. Children's toys littered the floor. He hoped and prayed that the intruder might stumble and fall in the plastic minefield but no such luck to be had.

"Sit on the couch."

Alton did as he was told. Ambient light flooded the living room. Only the bedrooms had curtains on the windows. Plastic blinds were a poor defense against the street light's perpetual glow.

The intruder dressed in black slacks and a white button down. He wore boots, like a farmer might use for field work. A wash of shadow covered his thin face. The revolver issued to Alton by the state now stared him down in his own home.

"Your name's Alton," James said. "Got a buddy named Henry."

"You know me, but I don't know you."

"Play your cards right, that may be as complicated as our relationship gets."

"I guess I don't mind keeping things simple."

"Henry went looking for Louis Hayte but he found salvation instead. Now I'm looking for Louis, and you're going to help me."

"What if I can't . . . help you?"

"You ought to think about your wife and your little boy. Let's say that you help me find Louis. Better yet, let's say my Ruth gets returned to me alive and breathing. Then there's no more missing persons case for the state police. No more strangers breaking into your house looking to tie up loose ends. Maybe you sleep better at night. And your family, they get to live. If you're lucky, so do you."

"You could just look him up in a phone book."

"Louis is a helluva lot smarter than that, Mister Alton. He knows I'm looking."

"Who are you?"

"I'm an angel sitting on your shoulder, helping you make good decisions. Your car is parked out in the driveway." He grabbed a set of keys from a hook by the door and threw them to Alton. "We're going for a ride."

"What if I say no?"

The intruder's demeanor shifted slightly. His shoulders were held back, his head forward and angled, as if astonished by the question. The left hand had been relaxed at his side, while the right aimed the gun. Alton heard the man's knuckles pop as he clenched his fist. The intruder lowered the weapon, but that didn't inspire relief.

Like being in a yard with a dog he didn't trust, waiting for it to jump and bite. Alton's suspicion wasn't that there was a threat of violence, inasmuch as the man before him was violence. Less a man and more like punishment made flesh.

"Say no to me." The intruder stepped forward. "I dare you."

Alton shook his head. He held out his hands. Words had trouble passing through trembling lips.

"I'll drive," he said. "I'll take you wherever you want to go."

Alton got into the car and the man sat beside him in the passenger seat. The automobile choked at first, and then roared to life. Alton fumbled around the steering column. Headlights scattered nighttime. The world beyond the windshield was an overexposed photo of phantasms threatened forever by dark vignette.

"Your buddy Henry must have a file. Something directed him to me. I want to see it."

The roads were normally busy, but the witching hour served as an exception. The city substituted stars with streetlights.

Uninspired constellations mapped the way for weary travelers.

This time of night scared away the god-fearing townsfolk, leaving only drunks and derelicts to roam amongst the false stars. The car headed west, and eventually the avenue curved north and merged with another street which took them further away from downtown.

Much less light in this part of town and the distance between streetlights grew much greater. The road twisted and turned. Passing cars were few and far between. They pulled up to a sizeable lot for such a meager station. Alton cleared his throat.

"We're here."

James sat in his seat. He made no sound nor gave instruction. Alton sat in the driver's seat with his hands on the wheel and eyes forward. The barrel of his gun rested against the back of his head. The sight above the muzzle tickled his right ear.

"You want I should park in the lot?" Alton asked.

"No, park it on the shoulder. In front of the station. Kill the lights. Shut it off."

"Henry's desk is just inside. Not a lot of troopers this time of night. But there'll be somebody manning dispatch."

"That's fine. I trust you have a key."

"Yes."

"Get out of the car. Stay in front of me. Try to run, try to dodge out of the way . . . and I will kill you. Then I'll drive back to your home and I will do things to your wife and child that would shatter your heart into a thousand pieces."

"I won't run."

"I know you won't. Now let's go."

Alton's heart beat hard enough to make him feel a little dizzy. His legs shook. The short walk through the lot allowed for reflection, mostly about his son and wife. He prayed in silence to Jesus Christ and God in Heaven.

I want to live, he thought over and over, *please, let me live through this.*

"You're shaking like a leaf," James said.

"The man working dispatch . . . he has a gun."

"Good to know."

"A revolver like mine, a .38."

"Well, that's why you're in front."

Alton stopped at the entrance. He fumbled around in his pocket and grabbed the key to the station. He held it up.

"We got a special knock for after hours, like a code. I got to do it before I go in."

"I won't abide lies, Mister Alton."

"I'm not fooling. If I just go in, I don't know . . . I don't want him to think something's up. Man is armed, after all. He may start shooting."

James weighed the reality of the secret code in his mind. He knew the fear Alton surely felt. Here the man yet stood and reasoned that he might wish away salvation by being an obedient parishioner. This man at dispatch, though, he may very well be holed up in this station, gun in holster, ready for action, a lone shepherd watching over sleeping sheep. Heathen rituals for righteous fools, their secret knocks and coded language, talismans hung on walls and worn around their necks, all a part of a foolproof plan to keep each other alive for one more day. Superstition rendered men reliably irrational, so Alton's claim stood to reason.

"Do it." James shook his head in disgust.

Alton tapped out the first five notes to "Shave and a Haircut." He and James stood there in silence. They waited for nearly a minute.

Finally, a light inside the station blinked twice.

"Okay, we're good."

Alton slid the key into the lock and the bolt snapped back. The front door opened wide. Darkness greeted them, and they accepted the invitation.

A weak, amber-colored glow came from the last room at the end of the dark hallway. Alton shuffled towards it. The nose of the revolver never left the small of his back.

"Stop at the doorway," James said. "Don't go in the room unless you feel me tap you with the barrel. Cough if you're getting this."

Alton cleared his throat.

"Who's out there?" A voice carried from the room. "Did you bring anything to eat? I'm starving."

"Sorry, Ed, I ain't got no grub." Alton came to a stop just outside the room. "I'm only stopping by to pick up some paperwork."

The office couldn't have been much bigger than a closet. The amber glow came from a cheap, plastic lamp that had been set on the desk next to the radio equipment. Ed leaned back in a wooden chair with his feet on the desk. A cigarette hung from the corner of his mouth. Even from the darkness of the hallway, James could make out the heavy bags under Ed's eyes.

"You hear from Henry?" Ed asked. "He never reported in after his shift."

"That's what I'm here for, actually. Following up on something he was looking into."

"Anything I can help with?" Ed laughed. "Get me out of this office, I'm begging you." He bolted up and out of the chair.

"Maybe you ain't heard, but there's a helluva fire north of here. Found Henry's car nearby."

"You don't say. Didn't find Henry with it, I guess."

James tapped Alton twice in the small of the back and Alton stepped into the office with Ed.

Ed crossed his arms over his chest and leaned against the desk. "Found nothing but fire, yet. And if you haven't heard from him, well, it don't look too good."

Gunshot exploded from the hallway.

Alton dropped to the ground. A .38 punched Ed in the ribs and he screamed in agony as he stumbled backwards. He couldn't see James in the dark, but that didn't stop Ed from grabbing his own revolver and firing off a round.

A lucky shot.

The impact knocked James backwards and winded him. He dropped the gun and it skidded across the floor into the darkness. Another blast from Ed. The round punched through the drywall not a foot from James's head.

Ed pulled the trigger a third time.

No bang.

Misfire.

Click. Click. Click.

James rushed into the room in the time it took Ed to look at the revolver and back at the doorway. He raised the gun to meet James's face.

James swept his right palm into Ed's wrist and grabbed the gun barrel with his left hand. He twisted the barrel away from him. The motion broke Ed's finger in the trigger guard and the revolver finally fired off another live round.

The bullet tore through the muscle in Alton's upper thigh

but missed the artery and femur. It exploded through the biceps femoris before lodging in the wall. Alton curled into a ball on the floor and screamed.

Ed's gun skidded across the floor and smacked against the wall. He looked at his hand and the ruined finger which dangled at an unnatural angle. His mouth hung open in shock.

James straightened the fingers of his left hand and threw a quick jab to Ed's right eye. The trooper rolled his head toward the pain. James pivoted on his right foot and used the momentum to drive a blow straight into the pressure point below the man's ear. Ed dropped to the floor. He was out cold.

Only seconds had passed. James assessed the room until satisfied that there would be no more surprises. This ridiculous charade was over. James knelt beside Alton.

"You're not gushing." James smiled. "That's a good sign. Still, we better get you a tourniquet. Don't need you passing out."

James pulled Alton's shirt off him and ripped it down the middle. He tied the makeshift bandage off above the wound. Alton watched as James crawled across the room and grabbed Ed's revolver.

Then James loosened Ed's belt and pulled down the unconscious man's trousers.

"What do you think you're doing?" Alton asked.

"I'm not doing anything. But you"—James stood up and aimed the gun at Alton—"you're going to take this man for a ride."

"The hell I am. Go ahead and shoot me."

"I surely will, Mister Alton. And when I'm done with you, I'll have your wife and boy. Cut one's head off. The other I'll ride from one side of your home to the other. Which one dies right quick and which one gets the business, well, I'll just have to make up my mind when I get there. Now, close your eyes."

Alton held out a hand in capitulation. He swallowed, hard, and his eyes watered and his brow furrowed in anger. He spoke through gritted teeth.

"I'll do it." He frowned at his own admission. He blubbered. "I'll do it if you leave them alone."

"Well, get on with it, you gimp bastard. I could baptize a dozen parishioners while you're fooling around."

The courtship, as it were, took Alton a minute or two of personal anguish before he got it up, but after that and a little spittle, he managed to do just fine. Ed didn't wake up, but he made a fair amount of noise. Busy dreams, no doubt.

"We want to escape ourselves," James said. "We're byproducts of waste. You slipped out of your mamma just like your wife's patch shit out a little turd and on and on. Heathens like you say seed and life. But I say we're just a different type of shit."

Alton's eyes locked shut. He clenched his jaw and his stomach flipped as if he rode a ride at the county fair. He wanted to stop but feared if he did this lunatic would kill him, kill his family. An orgasm rifled through him and Alton pushed through the horror of uncontrollable pleasure. He tried to stifle a moan. Instead, he sputtered as his body quivered and his leg throbbed in pain. Alton shook his head.

"I'll kill you for this." He cried.

"You are a patient man, Alton, to a fault, subservient." James walked to the office door and backed into the dark hallway until shadows swallowed him whole. "But I need you to hear me and I need you to understand. Damned are the meek. Damned, I say. They inherit nothing. You get home, you'll see I speak the truth.

And you'll know what to do."

James grabbed the loose paperwork off of Henry's desk. He stopped at the station entrance and listened as Alton anguished in the back office. He recognized the hymn and smiled. Those sour notes contained the wedded bliss of shame and relief, a song of a man reborn as a walking scar.

Billings waited outside and squawked in salutation. James patted his shoulder and the raven accepted the invite. The companions eyed one another. James sighed.

"My daddy used to preach that there was no pleasure but meanness."

"The man who cant do any hurt in this world cant do any good."

"Suppose you're right, Billings."

Morning light burned blue across the eastern horizon.

And James said, "Retreating night is like watching the birth of a great blue sea above our heads, and this dry earth below us is the bottom of that sea in which we drown each day. We should retreat until night falls. Our deeds will sow discord. This place will become an ant's nest disturbed."

Billings cawed in agreement and took flight.

James placed the revolver on the passenger seat in Alton's car. Then, he walked off to join Billings.

The two of them were gone before Alton managed to stumble into the parking lot. He used a coat rack as a crutch. His leg seeped.

Alton turned on the lights and sirens. The cruiser squealed away from the lot. The husband and father had no intention of obeying traffic laws as he sped home.

Alton plowed through the mail box at the end of his driveway and the car skidded to a stop in the yard. He thrusted himself out of the car and hobbled up the porch steps. He threw open the front door. Neighbors watched from windows. A handful stood in their lawns. No one approached the home, yet.

He shambled towards the bedrooms and shouted their names. He feared they would not answer, could not answer. Their absent response flooded him with terror. Silence was never more deafening than from loved ones.

Outside, neighbors drew closer to the home. A promise of spectacle attracted them. Alton's screams acted as honey.

"Oh, God." His neighbors heard him call out. "No."

His beautiful boy lay as stiff as a board in his tiny bed. Both eyes, lifeless, dotted with pinpoint hemorrhages. Bruises along the thin neck were a permanent shadow of the hand which strangled him. Alton screamed and ran to the master bedroom.

His wife still laid on her side, still faced towards the clock. Covers were as they'd been left, pulled to her shoulder, completely undisturbed. Alton could only mouth her name. He crossed to her side of the bed and the sight of her caused him to collapse against the wall. The man had opened her ear to ear, the wound a gaping maw, a raw and coagulated scream. Blood dried and thickened enough to appear black. The pool ran along her body, over the side of the bed and collected on the floor. Alton could see his reflection in the ichor mirror. Of course she had been cold that morning; she was dead before he ever woke up. It wasn't her distant breathing that he had listened to, but the breath of the one who'd killed her.

And then they spoke to him.

The air, that steady tempest, labored once more as a mournful wail outside the bedroom window. Two pained and restless spirits begged not for a house to haunt, but for the one they loved to join them. Alton, now, wanted everything to do with ghosts.

Neighbors watched him as he stepped out of the house. Some of them backed away. Folks closest together whispered to one another.

Alton reached into the car and grabbed the gun. Someone gasped. A few protested. But Alton knew what to do. The muzzle rested against his temple and he looked around at the faces of the damned. He let out a nervous laugh. "Ruth," Alton said, and then laughed again.

But no one understood his inside joke, and he blew his brains out.

Angels in nearby trees scattered in a pattern not unlike the material which exited Alton's skull. Those winged creatures never stopped their ascent. Blood and brains, however, became a veil which pulled taut and fanned out to its hem and then fell to the well-manicured lawn. Neighbors turned away. Those that had served in the war succumbed to crimson memories and phantom odors. And as his heart pumped its last, Alton lay sprawled across his front lawn and would never be any deader.

The sun crested peaks to the east and cast bright tendrils of unforgiving light upon the valley. Darkness retreated. Illumination pierced the deepest shadows and all the colors and shapes of Hell manifested like a shopworn apocalypse. James and Billings required something heavier than shade in which to hide. They spied their destination in the distance.

The erect steeple pressed high above the surrounding roofs and trees and violated the skyline. Atop the steeple sat the sign of the deceiver, a polished brass trap that lorded triumphant over all other deceptions, lulling the damned with the sweet meat of hope. No better charade than to hide from heathens by pretending to be a heathen.

Reverend Byron Manfred paced up and down the center aisle. His eyes darted, occasionally, to the vacated pulpit from where he preached. The pews were untenanted, though he liked to imagine them full of people, no more so than when alone. But, today, the church was an empty place of worship, a hollow stomach with high ceilings that contained exposed bones of pillar and ribbed vaulting. And Manfred, the audible growl of that empty belly, rehearsed the homily he intended for the coming Sunday service, until an interruption cut him off.

"They always suppoze they are learned, for they mistake rumors, skandals, and gossip for wisdom."

The unfamiliar voice startled Manfred. He turned around and expected a man, but found himself in the presence of a rather large black bird. The reverend took a step towards the beast. He intended to shoo it away, drive it to the door and back outside. But Manfred looked, really looked, at the creature. He stopped dead in his tracks. The bible he had tucked under his arm fell to the floor.

"What in God's name are you?" he asked in a whisper.

Billings stretched open his beak and cackled.

The large raven's eyes flashed a brilliant red, and then dimmed into such perfect points of light that the reverend forgot his question. The animal's skull, devoid of flesh, yet the bird stood before him. The impossibility of the cadaverous abomination robbed the man of his faculties. He leaned closer. Eyes the color of a red planet embedded in such darkness, beyond black, and if the reverend looked close enough, he could see those eyes pull in the color and light that surrounded them. But Manfred looked too long and went too deep. He forgot about the eyes and the raven to which they belonged. He forgot that he stood in a church and he forgot about his sermon.

Billings, then, tore away dull reality and gifted the wayward soul a revelation of immaculate loneliness. All the vastness and glory of Hell opened to the holy man like an atramental cloud. Nothing betrayed the reality of a prison quite like seeing it from the outside. And what an insignificant prison that pale blue dot seemed from that corner of the abyss.

Reverend Byron Manfred floated in outer space, far away from his church, far away from Earth, and from his fellow damned. He drifted out by the Kuiper Belt, at the edge of the heliosphere, where everything is a sunrise and a sunset simultaneously. In that vision, he watched all of the light in all directions and it shone like beautiful broken glass that had fallen for tens of billions of years, since the beginning of all things, that event which scientists named the Big Bang, and that which the false prophets coined Genesis. In that moment, Manfred saw through the heresy of light, the base wickedness of creation. Birth, itself, was damnation.

The true face of salvation was darkness, without form, and void. It called to him.

Then, Manfred realized no air existed with which to breathe. He fell back to Earth. Billing's gift of vision had ended. The reverend, reborn, released a primal scream. Billings retreated to the arched ribs above.

And then a new voice seemed to come from nowhere and everywhere, and declared, "The face of God is the darkest pitch. I see his face in the silhouettes and the shadows. True sight is no sight at all. There is no prejudice in the void."

James had snuck in during Manfred's journey and sat in the last pew. James, hands in lap, did not move. He offered no smile nor wave or any kind of salutation. He sat as still as a cat who's spied something of interest. But Reverend Byron Manfred pounced first and took James by surprise.

"I know you," Manfred said, as he righted himself. "It's been a long time, but I know you. Eyes like glass, like a robin's egg. You don't forget that."

Amused, James did smile, and beckoned. "Come, man. Sit with me," he said. "Tell me how it is that we are acquaintances, yet you I do not know."

Though the man he once was would have held reservation, Manfred existed anew, and felt no hesitation. After all, were they not prisoners, the two of them? Commiseration felt in order and he wanted to speak to this man like he'd never spoken to another, unencumbered by lies. He sat in front of James and leaned over the back of the pew, offering his hand. "Byron Abraham Manfred," he said. And they shook.

"And who might I be?" James asked.

Manfred pinched the bridge of his nose and wandered through his past. He smiled, and snapped his fingers. "I've got it," he said. "Your name is James. James Hayte. Beulah's your mother and Samuel your father, if memory serves. And a brother, I think, older boy . . . Louis."

Stunned, James held his hand over his mouth. His throat tickled. Eyes watered. He drew a sharp breath. "Remarkable," James said, and wiped his eyes. "I'm sorry."

Manfred offered the man a handkerchief. "Nothing to be sorry for," he said.

James took the cloth. He dried his cheeks and wiped his nose. "Thank you," James said. He held up the handkerchief in return.

"Keep it," Manfred said. "I've plenty more where that came from."

James smiled. "Appreciated," he said, and then stuffed the cloth into his breast pocket. "I've not spoken nor heard the names of my parents in many years."

"Neither"—Manfred added—"have I."

"But my parents never attended church."

"No, they were not members," Manfred said. "I only met them on two separate occasions. Once, your mother brought your brother here to be baptized, against your father's wishes, according to her. And I imagine he found out, otherwise I expect I'd have baptized you as well. The second time," Manfred paused and looked down, needing to collect himself. "You were very young, so I doubt you remember, but I came to your home and performed last rites for Beulah."

James leaned forward. "Yes," he said. "Of course." He ran his hands through his hair and laughed, then smacked his knee. He pointed to the reverend. "I dreamed about you for years, dreamed you were death and you took my mother. You chased me through many a bad dream." James leaned back, sighed in relief, and shook his head. "One of life's little mysteries solved by chance encounter," he said.

Manfred smiled at the sudden confession and its unexpected warmth. "Isn't that the way it always is?" he said, marveled by this turn of events.

"Tell me," James said. "With such a remarkable memory at your disposal, do you happen to remember my Ruth?"

Another memory flooded Manfred, then, with an urgency little felt outside of matters of life and death. Unease gnawed at his gut. Tension scrambled the chords of muscle in his neck. The man before him was *the man* he had been warned of, but the warning came so long ago as to have been dismissed. The young woman had entered the church, after service, to confess. She sought advice against those who would trespass against her. And she knew a day would come, in the future, when a man named James may come asking after her. How did she phrase it?

He means to be the death of me, she had said.

At the time, Manfred considered her fears a folly. Rare, indeed, were the men or women who truly meant murder. But here sat that very man. Death had come calling. He tried not to let on, but knew something had already given him away.

James sat forward and smiled. "You never saved anybody your entire life. Don't try to start now."

Manfred crossed his arms. The words he spoke, then, were not of Holy Scripture, though they were as dear to him, and appealed to him in much the same fashion. He said, "Life, although it may only be an accumulation of anguish, is dear to me, and I will defend it."

"You would defend a life besides your own?" James asked.

"I would," Manfred said.

James retrieved the gun that had been tucked into his waist band, and said, "Then I have a proposition for you, Byron Abraham Manfred."

Manfred ceased his comfortable lean and sat up straight. A cold sweat broke across his brow. His eyes fixed on the weapon. "You can't scare me," he said.

"Man preaches one thing but does another," James said. "Gather that about sums up your whole life to this point, wouldn't you say?"

"Shoot me if you must," Manfred said. "I will not break."

"No need to crawl up on the cross," James said. "I ain't gonna shoot you. What I propose is a game, maybe the last game you'll ever play. And you play it right, I won't bother you no more and you can take what you know about Ruth to the grave, so help me. That sound like a deal to you, reverend? Take a moment, if need be. Mull it over."

Manfred studied James. The reverend searched the man's steady gaze, the corners of his mouth, held taut, his cheeks slack, and he saw no betrayal of sincerity. Life, after all, revealed itself a game. The stakes were high every waking hour. Rarely, was one blessed with the opportunity to play in another's stead. If he could only save one more person during the course of his life, then he would save Ruth.

"May the best man win," Manfred said as he nodded to James.

James laughed. His cheeks blushed. The smile stayed on his face while he unloaded the revolver onto seat beside him. He held up a single round, and then he held it out to Manfred. "Examine, if you will," he said.

"I don't know much about guns," Manfred said. "Let alone bullets."

"Be that as it may, you have extended nothing but courtesy to me," James said. "In appreciation, I extend the same to you. If the caliber meets your expectations, however meager, then that is enough for me. I only wish for you to see that I am not rigging the game."

Manfred looked at the bullet in his hand. He rolled it between his fingers, tossed it in the air, and caught it. He bounced it against his palm. "I know this game we're playing," he said.

"You strike me as a learned man," James said.

Manfred, then, held the bullet out for James to retrieve. "I believe the name is Russian Roulette."

"Very good," James said. "I must say, you've been much more

engaging than the others."

The way he said it—*the others*—sent a chill through Manfred.

"Now, Russian Roulette is a game of chance," James said. "Most people put a single round in the cylinder, spin it, and you have a one in six chance of blowing your brains out. But that's not the way I play."

Manfred sighed. "I wasn't aware of any other way," he said.

"That round I handed you," James said. "That might just be your best friend in the whole world, right now. Might just be the round that saves your life." James balanced that round on top of the pew between them. "That brass bastard is the only one sitting out. You see, way I figure, one in six is for folks too afraid to play it my way. If I'm bellying up to the proverbial bar, then I'm playing like it is the very end. You beat five to one odds? Well, then, I wager the winnings are worth all the more. Ruth is worth a whole lot to me, do you understand?"

Manfred swallowed, hard.

"Hey now," James said. "Don't go yellow on me just because I upped the ante. The stakes were always high. You know that."

Manfred trembled. The convulsions were beyond his control. His breath, tremulous like a man at the end of hard labor, rattled from flared nostrils. "Since the stakes are high, may I be so bold as to suggest a consideration?" he asked.

James did not bother to look up while he loaded the cylinder. "Let me hear it, then," he said. He snapped the cylinder into place and spun it against his palm. When it came to a rest, he looked at Manfred and asked, "What kind of consideration are we talking about?"

"A coin toss," Manfred said. He reached into his pocket and pulled out a penny. "To see who goes first."

James crooked his mouth in contemplation. "Got nothing in that pocket a little heavier than a penny?" he asked.

"Penny's all I got," Manfred replied.

"Can I call heads?" James asked.

"You may."

James did not miss a beat. "Can I flip?" he asked.

Manfred wanted to say no. The word refused passage from his mind to his mouth. He sat in silence.

"I said"—James leaned over and took the coin—"can I flip?"

"No," Manfred blurted out. The reverend discovered a reservoir of courage. He snatched the coin from James, knocking the bullet from the back of the pew. It clattered against the wood floor. "You may call heads but I want to flip the coin," Manfred insisted.

James leaned over. "You're knocking over your friend, here," he said. "Ought to be more careful." And he placed the round back on its perch. James sat back and waved the man on. "As long as I get heads, then you can flip," he said. "We all got our superstitions."

Manfred did not wait for James to finish. He flipped the coin. The snap of his thumb against the penny echoed in that great, empty space. Manfred never took his eyes off of the spinning coin. James never took his eyes off of Manfred. The copper piece clapped against the reverend's palm and the man, in turn, smacked it down atop his other hand. Manfred beamed. "Heads," he said, and held out his hand to James. But James never looked at the coin, only at Manfred.

"So it is," James said. "Lucky you."

"But you didn't even look at it," Manfred said.

"There was no need," James said. "I see it in your eyes."

James held the gun to his temple.

"No," Manfred said and reached out—

Gunshot caused Manfred to flinch. Eyes shut hard. Ears rang. His nose flooded with the smell of the pistol's discharge and the unmistakable odor of burnt hair. The man felt reluctance to gaze upon his opponent and it took him a full minute to finally open his eyes.

James still sat upright, but slumped a bit to his left. Mouth hung open. Both eyes stared forward. One eye remained as glass colored blue. The other eye had become a whirlpool of blood with a black pupil at its center. The hair smoked at his temple and several lacerations spider-webbed from the impact like cracks in porcelain. Manfred expected a much bigger mess, brains and blood splattered all about, but it did not appear as though the bullet exited the man's skull.

The reverend waved a hand in front of James, and then he snapped his fingers. No response. Manfred clapped his hands together and raised them to the ceiling. "Thank you, Jesus!"

Billings cawed from above.

Manfred looked up and over his shoulder. The bird swooped down from the ceiling and came to rest atop the lip of the pulpit.

"I've had enough of you," Manfred said. He grabbed the revolver from James, left the pew, and marched up the aisle. "This is my house, and you are not welcome."

Manfred pulled the trigger—

Nothing happened.

Manfred held the revolver before him. He looked at the ugly creature. "Five to one," he said. "It's your lucky day, you unclean beast."

Laughter, then, filled the church, derisive and mean. Laughter dredged from the bottom of a pit, the mirth of gravel drowned in rot. The jeer sounded not unlike judgement being passed. Manfred knew the condemnation to be his own. He turned to face the angel that called upon him.

James stood at the other end of the aisle.

Manfred stammered. He stomped a foot down like a child. "How can you live?" he demanded. "How can you laugh?"

"If a man kan't laff there iz sum mistake made in putting him together, and if he won't laff he wants az mutch keeping away from az a bear-trap when it iz sot."

James raised his arm and pointed. "I took my turn."

Manfred turned red in the face and cried out, "But I won, damn you."

"Do an honest fucking thing." James said. "For once in your damned life."

"I beat you at your game, fair and square."

"One of the hardest men in the world tew kollekt a debt ov iz the one who iz alwus willing tew pay, but never reddy."

Manfred considered Billings' words. He held the gun to his head. The muzzle rested against his temple. "There's no virtue in this," Manfred said.

"Man is but living dirt," James said. "He assigns virtue to dirt." James crossed the distance between them. He placed a hand on Manfred's shoulder and squeezed. "You hunger—*thirst*—for righteousness and you're damned for it." James whispered into Manfred's ear, "You will never be filled." Then, James stepped away from the reverend and said, "That is your punishment here in Hell."

"Tell me, James," Manfred said. "Will I see you in Heaven?"

"When you reach the gates of Nihil, I promise you will see

nothing, ever again."

"Good." Manfred pulled the trigger. The hammer set off a live cartridge.

Byron Abraham Manfred floated in outer space, out at the edge of our Hell, and all of the light in all directions retreated, billions of years erased. In that moment, Manfred saw beyond light, beyond birth, to the unconditional love of impenetrable void, the embrace of her divine silence. Manfred had reached the gates of Nihil, and he would never be any deader.

James pulled the limp cadaver from the stretch of brain and skull and a pool of rich, thick plasma. After that, James took off his own clothes. Then, he stripped the deceased reverend and swapped outfits. The black suit and clerical collar left an immediate impression of respectability, as opposed to the soiled farmer's clothes in which he'd wandered into town. James wrapped his discarded shirt and pants around the ruined head to stave off further leaking. Then, he dragged the body to a closet and stuffed it inside.

James and Billings waited for evening. Sunlight shone through the windows on the south side of the church and turned simple stained glass into a kaleidoscope of lies. James admired the execution, even if he felt nothing for the fabrication. The Deceiver's mythologies unfolded in their totality through the succession of the stained glass windows, which began at the west side of the north wall and circled clockwise around the church. Revelations appeared above the entry. In that rose window, a beast the color of gold emerged from out of a sea of blue glass. James turned and looked to the pulpit at the gold-colored cross that adorned its face, and then back to the dragon that commanded the entry. James could not help but smile at their similarity.

Sunlight waned. Stained glass lost its luster. Shadows returned from their exile. James and Billings waited long enough. They let themselves back into the world at sunset. And that great stomach sat empty, save one rotting corpse, and hungered in the way in which all successful lies hunger, for belief.

Redness kissed the lips of the west and the east glowed like a ghost. Then James said, "The firmament never sleeps, Billings. One eye is always open, the other always closed. Day and night are an illusion meant to divide our better senses and rule over us. Time is a prison within a prison and the sun and moon are guards at the cell door."

James and Billings cut across the nearby cemetery instead of following the city sidewalks. No crowds to avoid within those rows of granite teeth. Besides, who looked more at home in a cemetery than a man dressed as a priest or a large, black bird? Neither would appear as strangers here.

Whistling caught their attention, though the sound seemed to come from nowhere. Not a soul in sight. Yet, the unmistakable notes of Stephen Foster's "De Camptown Races" floated along the sweet breeze. An arc of dirt in the distance gave away the tune's origin. Someone endeavored on behalf of the dead.

The gravedigger paid James no mind as he advanced the side of the deep hole. Nor did he notice Billings, who landed at the head of the grave. He kept to the job at hand. Whistling and dirt departed the earth so casually that one might forget the purpose of the hole.

James called down to the laborer. "How many graves, you reckon?" he asked.

The man ceased his whistle but kept digging. "Why, I wager about four-hundred fifty, give or take."

"I mean across the whole world," James said.

At that, the man stopped digging. He planted the spade into the dirt before him, rested a hand on top of the handle, and looked up. "Well, a hell of a lot more than four-hundred fifty," he said. "Lookin' pretty rough there, reverend."

"It's been a rough day, my good man," James said as he sat at the edge of the grave. Both legs dangled inside. He leaned back on his hands and gazed into the evening. "I read in a book what said there were men before us but history done forgot about them. I suppose all graves go unmarked eventually."

The gravedigger spit in the dirt. He wiped his mouth and said, "Show me one honest man among the spheres, let alone here among the regular folks. Sounds like hogwash to me."

"Maybe they had gods, too," James said, undeterred. "Maybe swimming out there in the cosmos is a great big grave filled with dead gods."

The gravedigger decided to take a step back from James. He put the shovel between them. His back rested against the wall of exposed dirt. He spit, again. "Give yourself to God, my pa used to say . . . or I can deliver you." His grip on the shovel handle tightened.

James rested his head against his shoulder and he peered down at the man. "I don't parry threats too well," he said. "But I do welcome them, if you think you're obliged."

"No threat," the gravedigger said. "Just wary of the tone is all. If I got to talk to someone, I like to know what in the hell it is I'm talking about."

"Understandable," James said. "The name's James, but you may call me Jimmy."

"Howard," the gravedigger said. "Phillips."

James surveyed the hole and the pile of dirt that sat adjacent its length. "Seems an awful lot of work for a thankless superstition," James said. "Burying the dead."

Howard crossed himself and said, "What I do is a mercy."

James raised an eyebrow. "Mercy for rotting meat?" he asked. "You overextend the definition, my good man."

"You sure you're a preacher?" Howard asked.

"I am, indeed, Howard." James said. "Best damn preacher you'll ever meet."

"You sure don't talk like Reverend Manfred."

"He and I preach a different sermon, that's no lie," James said. "Men like him lean too hard on the everlasting, the eternal spirit. There's no miracle in birth, to my eyes."

The gravedigger bunched up his face in confusion. He furrowed his brow. "Just what is it you do preach, then, if you don't mind me asking?" Howard said.

"I believe God wants us to die. God, himself, wants to die. Our endless worship keeps him going."

"If that were the case, then all that will be left is death." Howard reasoned. "Not so bad, I reckon." The gravedigger shrugged his shoulders and said, "Time's just a rope hung around all our necks, anyways."

"Given enough time," James said, then added, "even death may die."

Howard guffawed. "That's the kind of talk that'll end you up in a straitjacket," he said.

"Everything dies, in due time," James said. He pointed to the darkening sky and took on a tone of authority. "Even the stars die."

"That a fact?"

"Oh, yes," James said. "A star dies and seraph, like flies, set upon it and the corpse bloats, expands until electric maggots burst forth, then the bloat collapses, star-flesh spent and returned to the fertile void, the celestial rot. The other stars look on in wonder, asking, why does God let bad things happen to good stars? The other celestial beings whisper and their concerns are carried on waves of radiation. They ask the same thing you do. Why?"

Howard smirked. He shook his head and looked down at his feet. He laughed.

James, puzzled, cocked his head to the side. "Death amuses you, Howard?" he asked.

"Maybe you're right, mister," Howard said. "Maybe we are nothing. Maybe that's life's purpose. We just want to get back to zero—to square one—clean the slate."

"Now you're getting it." James said in triumph. "We *are* nothing, and we spend so much time creating a self, and then a facsimile of that, and then a facsimile of that, and so on and so on. There is nothing special in a beating heart. But, when it stops . . . well, that *is* something."

Howard placed a palm to his chest. "Love has to count for something," he said.

"Love?" James asked. "Love is no different than faith. Praying to God, telling someone that you love them, it's all a big fat sugar pill, an elixir meant to wash down bitter truth. Birth is a blasphemy. Death is the only miracle."

"See, that's where I draw the line," Howard said. "Sounds to me like someone did you wrong, and for that I am sorry. But I think life is so full of horrors that we just had to create love. It's like sainthood, you know, bestowing love on a person. They are the miracle in your life, and that is why you tell them you love them. Love, mister, love makes tolerable the horror of living."

"Ruth never wronged me," James said in a growl. "Louis stole her away. Death's the only miracle I have left."

James dropped down into the open grave. Howard gripped that shovel so hard he felt his fingers numb. Billings hopped back and forth in anticipation, but remained as yet unnoticed by the gravedigger.

"Death's no miracle, mister," Howard said. "And you are no preacher."

James looked up to his friend. "What say you, Billings?"

"If death iz an evil, birth iz a greater one."

Howard, surprised to hear another voice, allowed himself to look away from James and to the speaker. No man stood above, only a crow-looking bird, and a sickly one at that. Howard mumbled, "That's a nice trick."

"No trick, friend," James said. He took a step and looked for a reaction from the gravedigger, but Howard could not look away from Billings. "Though I will admit that truth can sound like magic when you hear so little of it," he said.

"A group of crows," Howard said, still looking at Billings. "You know what they call a group of crows? A murder."

"Unfair to the birds, I think," James said. "Though, my friend Billings is, in fact, a raven. Do you want to know what I call you? I look down from the mount and I see all of you huddled together and"—James leaned close enough for a kiss—"I call you a rape of corpses."

Howard screamed, though no one heard him besides Billings. Not that it mattered, because no one above would've been able to see him. No one could see the horrible violence that elicited such a piercing shriek.

James delivered the gravedigger to oblivion just as fast as his hands were able. He used the shovel to dig a smaller hole, like a small well, at the bottom of the grave. He slammed Howard's body headfirst into that hole. Then, he pulled the gravedigger's pants down below the buttocks. The handle of the shovel fed into the rectum for several inches, the muscle having relaxed in death, but came to an unseen blockade that impeded the advance. Undeterred, James leaned onto the spade with all the force of his weight until the handle found purchase and continued its journey. Satisfied, James crawled out of the grave, wiped his hands, and brushed the dirt off of his new suit. "No mercy for the merciful," he said. "Not in Hell."

The companions carried on their journey. Howard Phillips remained at the bottom of the grave he unknowingly dug for himself. And he would never be any deader.

Overhead, a flock flew southward, their formation the shape of a wedge, and silent. And James said, "The whole of this planet seems to be a great big sea. The way the angels of the deep and the angels of the trees move about may well be one and the same. Either creature serves to remind us of our limitations. Here we are, stuck in the middle of these waters, unable to rise or fall. Everything is a punishment, here, or a reminder that one is punished. No wonder, then, that the world is seeded with unrest."

"Contentment was born with Adam, and died when Adam ceased tew be an angel, and bekum a man."

James and Billings kept to the cemetery for a short while. The iron fence, though intimidating, its vertical spires topped with sharp and ornate finials, stood only waist high, so James managed to navigate his way over without snagging his clothes. The burial grounds abutted a small neighborhood filled with one-story homes that sat too close together, the kind of place that secrets went to die. James marveled at the rows of homes and their proximity. He looked back over the iron fence from whence they came. James saw those same rows and that same proximity amongst those granite stones. It struck him funny that people felt such apprehension about a graveyard, at night, as there were no greater ghosts than that of a community. Everywhere, prisons within prisons, the inmates rarely aware that when one door opened another closed and, sometimes, closed forever.

"Billings, you were once a man," James said. "Do you miss any of this?"

"I am too old and too respektable to be a phool enny more."

"Suspected as much," James said. "I will be honest with you, I look forward to being finished with this life."

"Finis iz the best and only friend that menny a man in this world ever haz, and sum day Finis will be the autokrat ov the universe."

"Honored, then, to do my part," James said. "However meager the role I've been given."

The neighborhood ran south of a wide runoff. They followed the twists and turns of the watery ditch until the modest suburb ended at a two-lane road that ran north and south. Across the street, a large park offered sprawl and safe haven. In the distance, mountainside glowed in the moonlight like a tide frozen in time. The desert lay beyond those peaks. James yearned for answers among that stretch of desolation.

The jungle gyms and swing sets appeared like bone sculptures in the nocturnal incandescence. An empty playground, its attractions and distractions unmolested by children, seemed a kind of tragedy, as if these playthings were monuments to innocence lost, or, a shrine that invited revelry as tithe to mortality. James had only ever been to a park once, before his mother passed, for a Fourth of July celebration. He remembered the day, clearly, in that way where memory and reality fold in on one another.

On that Fourth of July the men roasted a large pig and the smell of cooked flesh gave a taste to every breath taken. Tobacco smoke drifted but only so high that it hung as low clouds. The park swirled with activity like a gathering storm of fire and flesh. Conversation rumbled amongst groups while occasional laughter rippled across all parties and in that way mirth became as lightning.

A hush fell over the crowd when the first firecracker whistled through the air and burst in the sky. The explosion sparkled brilliantly but faded fast and left a thick white smoke in its wake. Sound and fury met with applause and for a moment the pork and flame gave way to the smell of rotten eggs. Each explosion dampened the air with a sulfuric ghost. A fiddler played amongst the crowd and as he played there were those who moved to his sounds as if under a spell. He played and he played and the people moved and high above an occasional star exploded and rained sulfur on the crowd. The men in charge of the pig drank away until the pig left their minds and they locked arms and danced while the pig became black. And the fiddler played and played. Women laughed and men stood arm in arm and the whole of them became as one and they cheered for the crackling lights in the sky and they cheered for each other and they cheered for reasons unknown to even themselves and then they became lost in their own memories and they cheered for those as well.

And the fiddler waltzed right through the crowd and straight to young James who did not partake but stood back and in awe. The fiddler smiled and nodded and played and no one paid him any mind at all except the young boy. An explosion of light and cheers from the dancing crowd and the fiddler released his instrument yet it played all on its own. Fiddle and bow hung in the air and the fiddler smiled at James while the fiddle played on its own. And the man who smiled opened his mouth and his innards were all aflame and James stood in awe but no one paid them any mind and the music took hold of them all and the pig turned to ash and the park smelled of sulfur and burnt flesh. The fiddler pulled at his golden sash and his robe fell open and exposed his form. White hair looked like smoke snarled in a gust and his eyes blazed not unlike the fire that burned beyond his smile. His feet were bronze and when he spoke it sounded like rushing waters. He held out seven sparklers in his right hand. His teeth were double-edged swords. The fiddle played on its own. The crowd danced. James held a sparkler before him yet could not remember where he got it and when he looked around he saw the fiddler walking away and playing but no one paid him any mind. He played as he went and he walked towards the lake and then on the lake atop the water and his music kept them dancing. They paid him no mind.

James wandered out of that memory and back into reality. He and Billings approached a white gazebo, the type meant to serve as a bandstand or a shelter for when it rained. A figure danced therein. She moved with grace. She did not yet realize that she had drawn an audience, for as graceful as she moved, James's airy gait was all the more, and his steps made no sound as he walked towards the pavilion. She danced unlike the haughty adults in his distant memory. Her movements were made with precision and quite formalized, her gestures grand though eloquent, her footwork intricate and often executed on tiptoe. She moved as if by song but no song played. James wondered what she heard in the recesses of her mind, and if those notes were as beautiful as her expression of them. So entranced by her effortless, soundless art, James had only just noticed the rope which hung from the ceiling beams and the footstool that sat below. She had tied a right proper noose for what could only be meant as her last performance. A rare production, to be sure, one that James planned to savor.

James called out to the woman. "When did you know you wanted to dance?" he asked.

To his delight, she did not stop dancing at his intrusion, but still humored his question. "The day I met the most beautiful boy in the whole world," she said.

"I see," James said. "A lover, I presume?"

"No," she said, flatly. "Mark was my son, my beautiful boy."

"And did he grow up to become like you?" James asked. "Is he an artist, too?"

"I believe he was an artist," she said. "But he did not grow up to become like me."

"Nor did I grow up to become like my parents," James said. "To their dismay."

"I harbor no disappointment in my son," she said. "He was sweet, and he was innocent."

"I see," James said. "And I suppose you plan on joining him."

"Loving the dead is a one-sided relationship," she replied.

"Loving the living is rarely any better," James said, and offered his condolences. "For what it is worth, I am sorry."

"Me, too," she said, as she continued to dance.

James braved a step closer towards the pavilion steps. "What happened to Mark?" he asked.

A pirouette and an arm bowed, hand held high above, she froze like a figure in a music box that needed winding up. "He hit his head and it cracked open his skull," she said.

Unfrozen, she abandoned the pose and bent at the waist.

"He died," James said.

She rose. "No," she said, arms held before her in a circle that met at fingertips. "But I never saw him speak again. I don't think he could." She spun like a top from one side of the stage to the other. "He had no control of his right arm and it stayed in the air, like he was forever keeping the sun out of his eyes. It was an uncontrollable gesture, but it was never erratic. It always contained a rhythm."

"I had it backwards," James said. "It was you who became like him."

"I wanted to picture what he thought," she said, "wanted to feel like he felt. Did that rhythm exist inside and out? That's what I wondered."

"You cannot hope to know the thoughts of another," James said. "You simply cannot."

"I'm inclined to think that his mind worked a lot like his limbs," she said. "His mind governed from chaos."

"As does God," James said. "But I chose to preach and you chose to dance, to die, dancing."

"Our bodies are so important," she said. "I mean, the body is the first fact of human existence."

"Everyone rationalizes the chaos in their own way," James said. "I think we call that process art."

"And, for me, the best way to use the body as a tool of art is to dance," she said. "Surely you have ways to navigate chaos besides preaching."

"I have a profound love of reading, even children's literature, with all its unabashedly stark metaphors. Mother was a bookworm and she passed the disease on to me. I believe the bridge between stories like Goodnight Moon and For Whom the Bell Tolls is relatively short. The outbreak of war or the need to succumb to sleep, both are profound enough to elicit the same response. We see clearly the things we love and cherish when faced with our own mortality. Heartbreaking and fantastic, such is life in this Hell."

"I'd like to make one last confession."

"Do tell."

"I killed him," she said. "In his sleep with a pillow. I couldn't bear seeing his eyes. Put him in the tub and made it look like a drowning. No one asked a single question but they knew. They knew I killed my boy."

"No, come on," James said. "What you did is something altogether different. Euthanasia, that's what doctors call it. It means . . . *good* death."

"Euthanasia is an excellent and comforting word," she said. "I'm grateful to whoever invented it."

"That, my dear, I do not know," James said. "But I can only imagine they set a loved one free, themselves, for why else coin the phrase?"

"If you love someone, you have to take them away from all of . . . this," she said, as she climbed on top of the stool. The dancer eyed the length of the rope which hung from the rafter above. She gave the rope a tug to test its hold. "Life is a nightmare," she said. "And do you know what you want more than anything else during a nightmare? You want to wake up." She fit her head through the end of the rope. The knot she fitted at the side of her neck, just below the ear and behind the jaw. She gazed skyward and said, "I'm going to wake up. Right now."

James stepped forward and gripped the handrail. He thrust out his hand. "Do you mind if I stay and watch?" he asked. He sauntered up the steps of the gazebo.

"I had hoped to do this alone," she said in polite protest. She smiled at him, defiant. "I'd like to own this, you see, to finally claim something as my own."

James kicked the stool out from under her.

"The pure in heart are as damned as anyone else," James said. "You'll be alone, soon, as alone as you've ever been."

The rope, though taut, did not snap her neck. The dancer thrashed. A catch at the end of her own hook, death the surface of the water of which she now swam. Blood vessels popped in both her eyes. Fingers clawed at the material around her neck and fingernails gouged skin. Blood ruined her shirt collar. She looked like a violent marionette.

"Kick your legs, you cannot swim," James said. "Swing your arms, you cannot fly."

Stockings soaked through from crotch to toes. Urine dripped to the floorboards. Her face ballooned and, first, turned the color of an apple, and then, the deepest shade of purple. Tongue swelled and pushed its way out the mouth. She made wicked noises, like heavy consonants of some guttural alien language. A full minute passed and then she quieted. Her hips thrust a few times as she rutted against death.

James counted the seconds between her every shrug and shake. The longer he could count between the spasms, the closer to oblivion she traveled, until she finally ceased her convulsions, and would never be any deader. James could not remember seeing anyone dance quite like that.

"What do you think about the woman's philosophy, Billings?" James asked. "That the body is the first fact of human existence. Looks like the last from where I'm standing."

Billings fluttered up into the rafters. He pecked at a web stretched between two boards. *"The reazon whi so phew people are happy in this world iz bekauze they mistake their boddys for their souls."* He caught a spider in his beak, but it crawled through a gap in his jaw and got away. Billings cackled and gurgled in anger. He hopped back and forth in a fit.

James laughed at his friend's comic misfortune.

And James said, "Living creatures of the earth fancy themselves as masters of their own fate. Seems to me that blind, stupid luck is about all any animal manages to conjure, as it stumbles from birth to death. Dominion lasts only as long as it takes to chew your food."

Billings voiced his displeasure with a low, gurgled croak.

"Don't hold back on account of me," James protested. "If you have something to say then say it."

The raven dropped down from the beams and settled on the railing. The bird ruffled his feathers, and then turned away from James. Looking back over his shoulder, Billings said, *"Brevity and silence are the two grate kards, and next to saying nothing, saying a little, iz the strength ov the game."* And then he spread his wings and took off into the dark distance.

"Come off it, Billings," James called after him. "I meant no effrontery."

James loitered beside the hanged woman for a quiet minute. He listened for his friend but only heard the wind in the trees and the gentle creak of the rope. The body moved, though barely, like the sullen pendulum of some morbid clock, or a wind chime made of meat. The sight was not unlike the last moments James had spent with his father, Samuel, in the big barn out behind their home.

"I'm off to join your mother," Samuel had said. And then the old man jumped from the ladder. The snap of his neck had sounded an awful lot like a walnut shell cracked open. He died a sight faster than the dancer, and swung back and forth in wide arcs. Young James didn't bother to stop the swinging, seeing as how it was the last thing his father would ever do, besides rot. Seemed only fair to James to let Samuel swing as long as he was able and, once Samuel finally stopped, James saw no reason to cut him down. Burying the body seemed a waste of good soil. By that point, no one else lived at the house, so no one else could tell him any different. Besides, the angels of the trees loved the easy meal, and James loved those creatures most of all.

James knew no such fate awaited the dancer, though, as she'd be cut down and whisked away just as soon as someone saw her hanging there, such a shame. Least she could do is be a meal, but no, she'd be thrown in a box and dumped in a hole. Even worms would go hungry. The only thing she'd feed was superstition, an overstuffed critter if ever there be. Fat and greedy superstition never wanted for a meal. Heathens spoiled their idolatries with a steady diet of fear, shame, and remorse. Every meal served in capitulation.

"Goodbye," James said to the corpse.

James bounced down the steps of the gazebo and headed in the direction Billings had flown. The park came to an abrupt end once James passed a copse of trees and he found himself staring down yet another small neighborhood, smaller than the last, to be sure, but still a source of possible annoyance. To his great happiness, however, this smattering of family homes looked to be the last. The town ended and a wide-open expanse spread from there to the mountains. James certainly felt a bit of solitary had been earned after having tended to so many parishioners. He headed down the dead-end street while his eyes darted back and forth. He suspected that Billings hadn't gone too far.

Shouts came from the last house on the left. Indistinct, clear in their anger, but not yet at a level one would associate with rage. A woman yelled something indecipherable. The tone sounded questioning and accusatory. Then a man responded with more of the same. Then another voice, much smaller, projected alarm at their outbursts, intoned concern that sounded parental. That third voice only reached the pitch of the other two voices in an effort to be heard. James kept his head low and quickened his step. These types of altercations were hard for nosy neighbors to ignore. If he hustled he would make it to the end of road in less than a minute or two. That empty stretch of darkness—of freedom from this town and its heathens—lay so very close.

And then a light came on, across the street, from a second-floor window. Others didn't bother with lights, though James could see curtains move in two different homes. If he hustled any faster, then he may as well make a run for it. But then all these people would be watching him instead of spying on their bickering neighbors.

Another light in a different house turned on, this one being at the bay window on the first floor.

James stuffed his hands in his pockets and watched his feet. He kept his pace. He pictured that inviting darkness in his mind. It called to him.

A storm door squeaked open, but James refused to look up.

Footfall sounded from the front steps of a wooden porch.

James could still make it.

There was still time—

"Hey, father," a man's voice rasped.

James kept his head down. He could make it to the clearing if he just went on and ignored the man. He watched his feet. He thought of darkness. Someone grabbed his arm. James spun around to see a wrinkled, balding man in a faded blue robe and matching slippers.

"Father," the elder fellow said. "Are you deaf or what?"

Out there, unseen, in the faraway dark, Billings laughed at James.

"I'm . . . my apologies," James said. "I'm in a hurry, you see, looking for my friend."

The man in the robe bent slightly and twisted his head towards James. "Damn, Father," he said. He stepped closer. "You been in some kind of accident?"

"An accident," James said. He thought about having shot himself in the head. He turned his good eye towards the fellow. "Accidents happen. We can't dwell on them."

"Hells bells," said the old man. "Well, maybe you can stop another accident from happening."

"My friend isn't from these parts," James said. He tried to smile. "I really must be going."

"Can't you hear that racket?" asked the old man.

"I think it is you, sir, who does not seem to hear me," James said. He pointed towards the dark. "My friend is out there, somewhere."

"Those two are going to kill each other." The old man pointed to the house at the end of the lane. "You got to do something. It's your job."

"My sympathies are presently with my missing friend," James insisted. He motioned to the house in question. "Their problems are not my concern, nor are they yours, my good man."

The old fellow harrumphed and looked down at his slippers, clearly disappointed and contemplative. He seemed to bob his head as if in agreement to some obscure thought that rattled through his own mind. He looked up and around, waved his hand in each direction he faced. Then, he stopped and turned towards James. He moved within an inch. The old man placed a hand on James's shoulder and said, "You can say that to me, but how will you look to all of them, if you leave now?"

James looked around. Neighbors stood at windows. Men and women, some alone, but some huddled together on their porches. Even the old fellow's wife, in a matching robe no less, waited at the front door of their home. A poodle cradled in the wife's arms, like a surrogate baby. All eyes rested on James, dog included. Each person waited to see if he would fulfil the promise suggested by his appearance.

James mumbled under his breath, "What good's a disguise if I don't use it?"

"Beg your pardon?" the old man asked.

James sighed. He made a sweeping motion towards the house. "Lead the way, sir," he said. "Give me an introduction and I'll see what I'm capable of doing."

A wide smile spread across the old man's face. "Hot damn," he said, and smacked his hands together. "They've been at it like this for months, couple of newlyweds. Guy's mother is older than I am, drives her crazy, the fighting. I knew stopping you was the right thing to do. Talk some sense into them." He took James by the arm and walked with him like that all the way to the front door. The smile never left his face. He gave James an exaggerated wink before knocking on the door. The fighting stopped. Not a peep for a moment or two. A curtain by the door flipped back and a man's face looked out, but only for a second.

"Goddamnit," said the man's voice from within. "See what you've done? Go get the god damned door."

The front door opened just enough for a small, old woman to peer out. She rolled her eyes. "Henry," she said. "Let me guess, we're keeping you and Margaret up? How many times must I tell you? Some people fight, and that's that."

"Edith, I found just the man to help you out in your time of need," Henry said. "Like a blessing, he came out of the dark just when you needed him most." Henry nudged James and nodded towards Edith. "Go on, father, introduce yourself."

"How do you do, ma'am," James said, and tipped his brow. "Name's James. But you can call me Father Jimmy."

"Henry, I want you to get off my fucking porch," Edith said. "And take this boogeyman with you. Mister James, is it? Henry and Margaret are just a couple of busybodies, is all, a great credit to your faith, those two."

"Edith," Henry said, cheeks flushed, his mouth hanging open.

Edith sneered at the old man. "And he'd do well to mind his own business," she said. And, having said her peace, she slammed the door. Inside, Edith spoke in a hissing anger and the man and woman whispered their apologies. Lights inside extinguished. Whatever transpired ended without fanfare.

Henry whacked the door, once, with his fist. "You're bringin' down the property value," he yelled, and then added, "you old bitch." Without a word to James, Henry turned away from the door and shuffled off the porch in a huff. A couple neighbors laughed before heading back into their own homes. People closed their curtains and turned away from their windows. Even Margaret and her poodle had already retired. It was an uneventful end to the neighborhood show. But it didn't have to be uneventful for everybody.

Henry closed the front door without ever looking back. He gripped the bannister and he pulled himself onto that first step, but the door's latch clicked as if someone turned the knob. The old man had never made it a habit to lock up, not in all his years, nor had anyone in his family ever locked up the house when he was a child. A locked door, then, simply never occurred to him until that very moment. A bit of night air shot through his legs and up the stairwell. Henry turned his head and as he did so, hands went to the back of his skull and under his chin, and his head did not stop turning until the vertebrae snapped and severed the spinal cord. Before the lights went out forever, he saw the face of Father James. Then, the very old and very dead man fell to floor.

A yapping bark caught James's attention. He looked up and saw Margaret at the top of the stairs. She grabbed at the dog's muzzle and shushed it. James went up after her. But he took his time. The woman's movements were laborious.

She ran around the corner of the landing and down the hall as if she'd never moved in that way before. The little dog growled with concern the whole way. Margaret's heavy frame and skinny legs failed to communicate in any beneficial way. Here, before James, went a woman meant for a comfortable chair, someone who had obviously never run from anything in her entire life. She even turned all the way around and backed into the room in which she thought to escape. Like her husband, and to the amusement of James, she failed to utilize the lock afforded to her. James opened the door, slowly, without entering the room.

Margaret continued walking backwards until her ass hit the far wall. She hugged the little dog against her bosom. "Please, don't hurt my dog," she said. She sobbed when James stepped into the room. Margaret tightened her grip on the animal when she saw the priest wringing his hands together.

"Peacemakers," James said. "Not satisfied with your own lot, you meddle in the tortures of others. You are damned among the damned. The Deceiver's children, that's what you are, doing his work for him."

James closed the door behind him. He walked across the room and opened a back window. "Billings," he said, his tone measured. He stuck his whole head out the window. "I've got some of that two dollar and fifty cent vermin you were so keen to see exterminated."

"Who are you talking to?" Margaret asked in a hoarse whisper.

James put a finger to his lips and said, "Please, Margaret, a person's last words are important." He looked at her like a disappointed parent. "Act accordingly," he said. "Think of something good. You have time." He crossed his arms and leaned against the wall.

Wings flapped in the distance. The sound got closer and closer until, finally, Billings landed on the windowsill. His eyes filled the room with light.

Margaret gasped. Her hands went to her mouth. The small poodle slid down the front of her and spilled to the floor. As soon as it regained its footing, the beast set to barking, short and shrill little sounds, all that its tiny lungs could muster.

James scooped up the poodle and smacked it on the nose. It yipped, once, and shut up. "Margaret," James said. The woman couldn't take her eyes off Billings. "Margaret," James said, again. He snapped his fingers and gave a little wave. She noticed, but now her eyes darted back and forth from James to Billings.

"Good enough," James said. "Where's your bathroom, love?"

"That bird"—Margaret pointed—"his eyes . . . his skull."

"The bathroom, Margaret," James said. "I'd like to put the dog somewhere safe."

Margaret waved towards the door without taking eyes off Billings. She mumbled, "Down the hall."

"Name?"

"Margaret."

"No, my dear, the dog."

"Where's its skin?" she stammered.

"Hopeless," James said, exasperated. "Billings, I'll be right back. Watch this one and make sure she behaves."

James walked out of the room. He held the dog like a football, tucked against his side between his hand and elbow. The bathroom door stood open. A white, clawfoot tub sat at the far end, beneath the small frosted window that faced the noisy neighbor's home. James placed the poodle in the tub. He patted it on the head and the dog licked his hand. "Be right back," James said. He closed the door, but instead of heading straight back to the bedroom, he detoured down the steps to the first floor. He wandered to the kitchen where he grabbed a steak knife, then back to the steps. He kneeled down and cut out Henry's eyes.

"I owe you a meal," James said, as he entered the bedroom. He tossed an eye through the air.

Billings caught the eye. The raven leaned his head back very far and the eye fell into the pit of his body. The bird gurgled a happy sound and he gave a small hop on the windowsill.

"What do you think of peacemakers?" James asked of Billings. "Busybodies are all they ever are to me."

"Wouldn't hesitate tew stop a phuneral procession to ask what the corpse died of."

James tossed Henry's other eye to the bird.

"Sweet Jesus," Margaret gasped. "It talks?"

"Fitting last words, Margaret," James said. He looked around the room. A copy of Gone with the Wind sat on the bedside table. James walked over, picked up the book, and used it to beat Margaret to death. Then, he cut out her eyes, too.

"There iz a great menny folks in this world who are like little flies; grate bores without meaning or knowing it."

"Well, you'll get no argument from me, Billings," James said. He held up Margaret's eyes and shook them like dice. He smiled and said, "But that's no reason to be mean to their dog." James marched back down to the bathroom. He opened the door and the little poodle stood on its hind legs, panting, and the animal's stub tail wagged so that the whole dog seemed to dance. James dropped Margaret's eyes in the tub. The dog promptly ate both. And James smiled, patted the dog, and lifted it out of the tub.

James surveyed the neighborhood from the large bay window in the living room. No yelling. No lights. Now, the hour was very late. The street seemed, for all intents and purposes, quite dead, though not quite like Henry and his wife Margaret, who would never be any deader.

Poodle, raven, and man snuck out into the hour and headed for the mountains. Strips of moonlight cut through the spaces between dark clouds. Snatches of earth colored like a frozen lake by those slow-moving spotlights. Billings flew, sometimes gaining too much ground, but he always circled back to the group. The poodle trotted alongside James just as happy as if they'd been together for years and years. James, though pleased with the company, gave only passing attention to either. He locked his eyes on the mountain ridge, that wall that separated him from Louis and, more importantly, from Ruth.

They managed to hide for a long time but not even these mountains could stop what was coming. And while James knew every step brought him closer to her, the walk was not unlike the dreams he had where he would run in place while his destination stretched further and further away. Only, this was no dream, yet, as he walked, the mountain ridge seemed to grow higher and higher, and swell like the backs of demons that had turned their asses to him. But no demon—nor man or animal or any other lost soul—could stop him.

And, as it often happens when walking through Hell, James spied a fire. The light appeared small, but like the mountains, it grew, and what an inviting color to see amongst the blue. Yellow and orange sliced through gloom like a sword. That light, like the light of Empyrean, promised baptismal warmth. James thought about everything he'd seen and done since leaving the green church, his roving sermon and the souls delivered, all of that good work. And James said, "I'd like to rest." He looked up, but Billings had flown too far ahead to converse with. When the raven circled back, James called out, "A fortunate accident, Billings." And he pointed in the direction of the distant fire.

"Thare iz no such thing az acksidents, if one thing happens by acksident awl things may; Heaven haz no beureau ov acksidents."

"Such wisdom, Billings," James said. "I do envy your insight."

Not one half of an hour passed and the three of them arrived at what revealed itself to be a campfire. A man greeted them, warmly. He dressed as James had dressed, clerical black and a white collar, so when the men sat across from each another, the sight had all the earmarks of their gazing into a mirror.

"Funny," James said. "Two priests meeting like this."

"Kicked me out of town," said the priest. "Drove me out of my own church."

"Must've been a good sermon." James chuckled. "Too much truth will get you in trouble. No one wants to hear it."

"People don't want to hear what they already know in their hearts," said the priest. "They think me mad. The mad priest, they called me. Pot calling the kettle black."

"Death, I tell them, is a miracle," James said. "The only one that really exists."

"Not bad," the mad priest replied. "I preached similar, but the sermon what got me in real hot water was on Adam and Eve."

"Do tell."

"Well, I started thinking, you know, that Eden, it weren't no place. No real place, I mean, on a map and such. Got me pondering what else might be wrong with all of it right from the start. So I put it to the congregation. Eden wasn't a place, the tree were no tree, and the fruit was something altogether different. I said, what if the tree of life, what if that tree was just Adam's cock, and his semen, that were the fruit. The mouth of which Eve ate of the fruit was her cunt, and the two of 'em gave birth to the first death. You see, Eden *was* Heaven, and we've just been wandering Hell ever since."

James leaned back and laughed. The sound of his delight echoed off the mountainside. He sighed and wiped his eyes. Then, he clapped and rose to his feet. "Bravo, sir," he said. "Your congregation must be loaded with fools if they cast you out for that." James leaned forward and put his hands to his knees. He said, "I have no disciples, mad priest, but I'd like to see you keep that sermon alive. Tell it to whoever will listen. Like me, you're damned for your righteousness. You and I, we have no kingdom, here or hereafter. There is only a return to oblivion."

The mad priest stared into the flames. "It's a lonely sermon, isn't it?"

James glanced at the raven, to his left, and the dog at his feet. "Doesn't have to be." He picked up the poodle and walked around the fire to the mad priest. "I have the raven," James said. "You can have this dog, as long as you promise to treat it well." He held out the animal.

The mad priest beamed. "Till my dying days," he said. He held the little dog in his lap and petted it like a child would. He spoke to the animal as some folks are inclined to speak to babies or small children. The dog turned its head, inquisitive, and wagged its tail stub.

"Now, if you don't mind," James said. "I plan on sleeping a spell." He lay on his side with his back to the fire. He listened to the man's voice as he spoke sweetly to his new companion. Then, James fell asleep and did not dream, did not stir, until the sun rose above the ridge.

When James woke up, the fire had died and turned to smoke, though the ashen logs still gifted a bit of heat. Billings attacked something in the field, not too far away. And the mad priest and the dog still slept, huddled together, and in that moment they struck James as being quite helpless. He felt compelled to offer them some bit of security, so he took the revolver from his waistband and sat it close by. There were only the three bullets left, but if the man had a steady aim, then each shot could procure them a meal, by hook or by crook.

"I hope I didn't make a mistake"—James walked towards

Billings—"leaving the poodle with him."

The raven had bested a locust and made breakfast of the insect. *"Life iz sweet, and it iz cheaper tew hav it saved by a dog than by a doctor."*

James and Billings left the basin valley by the only means left to them. Up the southern ridge they climbed and many hours passed. The higher they climbed, the thicker the trees grew, and James couldn't help but think of his green church, and how he missed it so.

Shadows crawled about and after several hours shadows darkened, until all the wooded mountainside existed only as shadow. Billings, then, lit their way with his radiant eyes, which drenched the immediate surroundings with aurorean waves of ruby red. The two of them reached the summit in time to bear witness.

Sun, in the west, crawled below the mountain ridge. Dying light cast those westward mountains in silhouette, transformed peaks into black teeth in a mouth as wide as one could see, a mouth that was set like a bear trap ready to snap shut and crush the life within. Complete darkness shrouded the city in the valley below, which sparkled with artificial stars, a poor reflection of the firmament. Moon, in the east, an eye robbed of all signs of life, an orbital bone covered in porcelain dust, blind to what passes before it, and forced to forever chase the setting sun.

Empyrean burned to the north. James hoped that the beacon would never be extinguished. As it were for the angels of the trees, this journey south need only be temporary. He had no plan other than to return home once he found Ruth.

From that summit, in every direction, lay all the kingdoms of the world and their glory.

"The deceiver was right, you know, to abandon this," James said. "For all his lies, even he knew there was no worth here. Poor, stupid creatures, I pity them."

"Pitty costs nothing—and aint worth nothing."

"Yes, I know. They wish to live forever and were promised eternity as reward. It is not their fault that they are blinded to truth, then. Nor does it surprise me when they fight against it."

"Truth iz the edict ov God."

"They can barely face their own mortality, yet God demands a return to silence that can only happen when all parishioners embrace oblivion. They scream when they're born and they scream when they die. Most have never known a moment of real silence."

"Silence iz venerable; if thare iz enny thing older than the Creator, it must hav bin silence."

James and Billings pressed on. Sun rose and the two took to some lean shade offered by a twisted, dry tree. Billings swooped down on an unsuspecting jackrabbit. They ate the raw meat and kept to that shade. After midday, they returned to their march. Night fell and James slept while Billings watched over him. They embarked early the next morning, finally reaching Adel by lunchtime.

James walked into the small town's single diner. He managed to arrange a sandwich in exchange for some small labor, dish washing, mostly. The owner, a slim man with a high back and crooked neck, asked if James were replacing the minister who'd gone missing about a year and change prior. James looked down at himself, having forgotten about his disguise. He felt the clerical collar around his neck and grinned. "I'd not heard anything about that, no," James said. He decided to play up his role of shepherd. "Tending to another matter, you see. I've been sent by relatives to inquire about the unfortunate death of a farming family."

"The German fella," the owner said, disapprovingly. "I knew him, had a young wife and a boy. Bad business, that. Locals think injuns done 'em in. You ask me, it was the surveyor done killed the jerry and his kin. Killed his partner, too."

James perked up. "Surveyor, you say?" he asked. "Do tell."

"Yeah, they came through here, rented horses from a local rancher," the slim man said. "Last I saw, they were heading out of town on horseback. The one feller done killed the whole bunch. Still out there, too. They ain't found him by now, likely never will."

"I'd like you to do me a kindness," James said. "Show me, on a map, the whereabouts of that farm." James made sure to smile, and added, "Please."

He retrieved a folded map of the state from his tiny office. Together, they pulled that map open and smoothed it across the top of a linoleum table. The owner grabbed the pencil tucked behind his ear and drew an X over a spot just southeast of the town. He tapped the X and sat the pencil on the map. "That's the place," the owner said.

"The surveyors," James said, his tone ponderous. "Were they, by chance, accompanied by a woman?"

"Those two?" the owner asked. He laughed. Both eyebrows arched high and he took a deep breath through his wide, red nose. "Don't think they had much interest in women, those two. They were a couple of real Sodom and Gomorrah-types, if you cotton to my meaning."

"Impossible," James said. He shook his head. "Louis . . . he stole my Ruth."

"Took your what, now?" the owner asked. "I thought you said you were out here for those dead Krauts."

James calmly reached down and took hold of the pencil. "Are you saying Ruth wasn't good enough for my brother?" he asked. His voiced carried a tone of accusation. "How *dare* you talk that way about *my* Ruth." He stuck the owner in the stomach with the pencil in two quick thrusts.

The slim man doubled over. His hands instinctively went to his midsection. "You stabbed me," he said. Blood blossomed like spilled watercolor across dirty canvas. "You goddamn sonofabi—"

James sunk the pencil through the man's cheek. He cried out but James silenced him with a boot to the gut. The slim man fell backwards, and James grabbed him by an ankle and dragged him into the kitchen, where he stabbed him a few more times in the neck and face, occasionally the hands. James tired of the flailing arms. He stood up and brought a boot down onto the owner's head until the skull collapsed and poured its contents across the tiled floor. What life the man had left gurgled into the nearby drain. The mess reminded James of a plate he had cleaned earlier, smeared corned beef hash soaked in ketchup.

James grabbed the map and left. Billings soared high above until they were both well out of Adel. Day became evening and the blazing eye drooped below its westward lid. As the orbital bone of nighttime crowned in the east, the two approached a single tree as they headed southward. James passed that desiccated assemblage of limbs without a thought, but Billings remained perched on a high branch and let loose a shrill call. James turned towards the tree and saw his friend had changed.

Billings, once black, his feathers now blanched. Each quill appeared within a shade of pale not terribly removed from his bony head. And the eyes, which had burned fierce, lost their respective flares and now simmered a deep blue. Whatever fire birthed him presently diminished, and he looked as ash.

James harbored the disappointment which precedes loneliness. "I suppose this is where you leave me, emissary from Empyrean," he said.

Billings bowed his skeletal head and cawed in affirmation.

"Then it has been a pleasure, Mr. Billings, to have had your company."

"Pleazure iz like a hornet—generally ends with a sting."

"Tell me, Billings, do you see the future?" James asked, succumbing to a deep melancholy. He cried, "Am I ever to be reunited with my Ruth?" He ran to the tree and reached out to his friend. "Let your parting words be my fortune," he said, all but begging.

"Love feeds on hopes and fears, and, like the chameleon, takes its color from what it feeds on." Billings sprang from his branch and took to the sky. He cawed one last time, then said, *"There is no revenge so komplete az forgiveness."*

And then Josh Billings, he of hollow bone and old voice, one and only friend to James Hayte, erupted into flame. The raven deteriorated as it soared, an incinerating flight, while crematory ash fell like so many blistered fireflies, a great ribbon of luminance. Each separate dying ember wrought its ghost upon the desert floor.

The individual coals burned a warm color of orange and they sizzled not unlike sparklers, so popular with children during summer festivities. The last ember floated close enough to James for him to hold out a hand and catch it. Both light and heat expired as it touched his palm. Extinguished with a heavy sigh, the little ember turned black as coal.

The charred remain of his companion crumbled to dust and

scattered in the wind. James watched the cloud of meager remains swirl as it spread out and over the distance until all that remained existed as little more than a hint of movement, which quickly faded into the silhouettes and shadows of desert landscape.

A strange voice called out and the hair on the back of his neck stood on end.

James.

He spun around.

Four feral ass lumbered out of the darkness. Bestial eyes shone like wet, black lacquer. Guttural snorts preceded their two-toned brays, the wanton lechery of famished demons in an atrophied Hell. Sanctuary welcomed their savage benediction with open arms for he felt as little fear of these creatures as he did any parishioner. The five of them bellowed their hymns. Each ecclesiastic proselytized laceration. Death suffered adulation. The missionaries clashed. Singular cultures forced upon one another like a violation. Obscure theologies met with crushing blows and the gnashing of teeth. Faith held steadfast against faith.

And blood shone black in the moonlight.

PART THREE

Four men, myself included, set out to find the remains of my father and track down the man suspected of killing him, a fellow by the name of Louis Loving. Never did find Louis. Don't suspect anyone ever will. Instead, we found something so much worse.

Wish to hell we'd never gone out there.

I had a responsibility to the three men I took with me into the desert. Owed my dear friend most of all, but the others demanded a debt as well. A good man ought to have every intention of paying back what is owed. And once delivered, I could attend my own grave matters with a clear conscience.

No way to forget what transpired during that long night. I dare any man tell me he could. Who would possibly believe any such thing without experiencing the perversity themselves? Only recourse seemed to be one of embrace and acceptance.

Knew but one way to reconcile all what come before. I set about to preparing reparation. Only when amends were made, in full, could I dare go back to that darkness.

I wanted to see him again.

***

My childhood friend Daniel Loving entered the world during a red evening in a late spring, according to my father. Nineteen Forty. Danny's mother, Ruth, delivered the boy at a very young age when her heart still loved poetry, as she'd said on more than one occasion. Like a second mother to me. She often recalled that Danny seemed to be born searching. His father said little to, or of, Daniel.

Louis Loving cared for the boy and his wife but kept his emotions private. Man extended affections to my father but rarely anyone else. His love expressed itself through his distance, or so he thought. Danny grew up a wild youth because of this though his mother's affections informed his actions, so, wild but not entirely reckless. Young man became a good fisherman and a skilled hunter. He learned to fight. And he believed these trades would make his father love him.

In all of the many things young Danny did, or set out to do, he searched most of all for a love which seemed missing. In all things, I believe, Danny spent his formative years searching for his father. And so, Danny's affections were scattered like stars and, like stars, he seemed to wander when he became of age to do so. He never did wander too close to me. I'd have let him if he ever wanted, but we were not alike in that way. Eventually, his affections bought him no small amount of trouble in the form of a young woman's growing belly and her aggrieved father, so Danny thought leaving town for the best. Though we'd grown apart, I found him work on a ranch not one day's distance and for several months he earned keep and meant to save as much as possible in the hopes of making right the situation at home. But bad news cut his plan short and Danny found himself on the road back to Klamath Falls.

Word travelled over the mountain ridge and to that ranch that Louis Loving had gone missing and maybe worse. I sent the letter myself. But I forged his mother's signature. Knowing Danny as I did, I knew he'd return for Ruth before he ever came to my beck and call. And his father, in a relative sense, had always been missing, so nothing new there.

I intended to settle the matter of my father's murder, and I meant for Danny to be by my side when it happened. We'd already grown distant, and I knew if I acted on this by my lonesome that a gulf would come to divide us for our remaining days. Raw as my heart may have been, I simply could not have that.

In the day leading up to Danny's return, memories washed over me of this place where we grew up. Events and ages of our respective times crisscrossed one another like a life lived all at once. Not a year had passed since he left, but my recollections seemed so far away from my present state of mind, and so removed from the life he'd since chosen to live. Childhood crushes, scraped knees, learning to drive, fights with father and mother's tears, all of it may as well have been a stranger's memories. But they were mine and I knew it. Why else would they hurt so much?

The sun finally fell beyond the horizon. A lack of light offered me some small relief. Wasn't sure how much I wanted to see quite yet. If memories of Danny taxed my heart to such a degree, then the reality of seeing him might just have devastated me. Somber shadows acted as balm for the queasy homecoming. I felt thankful for the dark.

And nighttime is kind to Klamath Falls. The city sits near the river and its businesses and houses pepper the basin valley like wildflowers fed by the currents. After the sun does fall down, all the telling details of a hard-living town vanish amidst the glow of artificial light. Even an ailing tree can have a kind of majesty when wrapped in colored lights in a darkened room. A city is no different.

Downtown Klamath sprang from the riverfront and ran

towards the hills to the north. There were a handful of bars within walking distance of the Link River Bridge, which Danny would certainly cross as he came home. And I suspected his arrival. The owner of the ranch rang me up and let me know Danny took off. I had a strong suspicion he'd end up in Peterson's bar. Place had been our fathers' old haunt, after all. Booze would help ease through the feelings, of which I'm sure he had as many as I.

And though eager to see my friend, I carried with me no small sense of defeat as I made my way into the darkest and most deserted of the downtown watering holes. I sat in the corner, in the dark, as far from everyone else as possible. There I waited and hoped in vain that no violence would come of my machinations.

Handful of men sat at the bar itself. Three more played pool in the back, adjacent my dark corner, but they paid me no mind at all. An older woman sat and fed a bobcat chained to the end of the bar nearest the entrance. She made baby talk to the animal. No one else said anything. And no one looked familiar. Wouldn't be the first time I felt like a ghost in the very town where I grew up.

Nicotine hung heavy in the air. So did suspicion. It'd been years since I had a smoke. Rolled my own when I could, but rolled my last after an uncle was chewed apart by cancer. I sucked in and tasted the air and hated to think I'd have to make do with the second-hand variety. But I couldn't imagine asking to bum a smoke from anyone in Peterson's bar.

"No sir," I whispered.

Then the door cracked open and my heart jumped. He didn't see me, and I found myself at a true loss for words. Daniel sat several stools away from the nearest drinker at the bar. He nodded to the bartender. And the bartender shuffled over and leaned on an elbow and delivered some side-eye to the young man.

"What's yer poison, Mac?" asked the bartender. The lanky fellow wiped a glass with an off-white rag. He flashed a smile right about the same color. Bad teeth made Danny uncomfortable and he unconsciously ran his tongue across his top teeth and gums.

Danny leaned forward when he spoke and offered a grin. "Buy some smokes?" he asked.

"Sure," said the bartender with a nod.

"Okay to smoke in here, I guess?"

The bartender raised an eyebrow and motioned around the establishment. "Don't put it out on the bar or the floor," he said. The bartender grabbed an ashtray from beneath the bar and set it in front of Danny.

"Fair enough," said Danny. "How late are you open tonight?"

"Shit," said the bartender with a laugh. Then, he spoke up for the whole bar to hear, "I guess maybe when I close depends on how much I'm selling." He looked around but none of the patrons seemed to give him notice.

Then, one of the fellows at the end of the bar laughed a little, a glimmer of mirth.

"Gimme your cheapest beer," said Danny.

Bartender shrugged his shoulders. "We only got but the two kinds," he said.

"Whatever costs less," said Danny. "I'm not picky."

"Bottle okay by you?"

"Bottle's fine."

"A'ight, then," said the bartender, and he crossed his arms. "Sixty-five cents, Mac. A bottle of beer is cash up front. Too many try to run out on a tab."

Danny reached into his pocket. "I can do that," he said, and tried to work out a loose bill. Unfortunately, and quite by accident, his entire savings spilled onto the floor. He may as well have shattered a glass or banged on a piece of metal siding.

I didn't make a move, then, though I should have. Knowing I had my knife on me set my mind at ease a bit. And Danny was always good for a show. He had fast hands, stronger than he looked, too.

If he didn't have everyone's attention before, he surely did after seven months' worth of earnings hit the ground. Every fellow in the bar watched as young Danny picked up his cash. Only person to pay him no mind sat up front, feeding a wild cat. All those men, even the bartender, made eyes at Danny the way that bobcat looked at the old lady who fed it.

Peterson's bar only had the one entrance. Danny surveyed the room and I held my breath. I think he saw me but I couldn't have looked like much more than shade dressed in clothes. I wasn't as antsy as the rest, either. Two guys, younger than everybody else and probably looking to live it up, correctly surmised this was not their crowd, so they beat feet. Their exit left but one other guy at the bar. Then there was the lady jabbering to the goddamned cat. Two of the guys playing pool must've gone into the john. The third guy in that party leaned on his pool cue and stared towards the bar and probably at Danny, since Danny had an unfamiliar face and, apparently, a lot of money.

Or, god forbid, the fellow recognized him. After all, Rae's daddy had supposedly offered a reward for the man that knocked up his little girl. People do all manner of crazy things for money. And love.

So, that was a total of six, which included the barkeep. I figured the number could probably be whittled down to five, since the old lady didn't seem to be a part of their little universe…or anyone else's. And it made no sense to include the bobcat, chained as it was.

The guy at the end of the bar, who chuckled to himself, he got up all casual and sauntered up to the entry and took a seat by the door. Danny, clever as ever, pretended not to notice. He tapped the bar and said, "I think I'll take another beer." Danny never carried a weapon, but I've seen him knock a man unconscious with a bottle on two separate occasions.

Like a lot of dive joints, the place was long but not wide. The bar itself ran a good sixty feet and probably sat a lot of thirsty folks on a busy night, but this was late Wednesday in a blue-collar town. Busy nights kept relegated to Fridays and Saturdays, while the rest of the week went to the hardcore drinkers and dealers. Depression and bad intentions patronized a joint like this on off nights.

What light the place had going burned low enough to make rotten decisions look like great ones. The floors consisted of dark wood and a rough finish, typical of a place like Peterson's. Probably saw its fair share of beer and bodily fluids. If a community had a magic mirror, it was the local dive, the dark corner of a city's soul.

That fellow still sitting by the entry, he didn't try to hide the fact that his eyes were trained on the kid with too much money in his pocket. No good would come of trying to run for the door, so Danny drank his beer and waited and watched and wondered when the fight would kick off. When that beer finished, he drank another and waited a while longer. I waited with him like a guardian angel. It wasn't the first time, didn't figure it being the last.

Near half an hour passed before our patience seemed to pay off. One of the pool players walked up to the bar and tapped on

Danny's shoulder. I didn't think to draw my knife and I didn't want the attention. I doubted one fellow would pose much of a problem. Couldn't guess how long it'd been since I'd seen my friend in a fight.

Danny saw the fist and immediately scowled as he turned around. In that moment, he wasn't even one-hundred percent sure whose fist flew at him. Not that it mattered. He'd find out soon enough. And as long as it remained one-on-one, the fight ought not to be a problem. He wouldn't want to have to take on a bar full of bored drunks, but he worked too damn hard for that money. I'm sure he didn't plan on giving it away for free. Not that I'd let it come to that. I just hoped to hell no one in there was packing.

Danny leaned back, but not far enough, so he rolled with the right hook and let those knuckles slide off his left cheekbone. The punch would've done a lot of damage if it'd made full contact. A fist clocked to the head isn't at all like on television or in movies. Fists always hurt, every time, though if you get socked enough then you have a better chance of taking the blow and moving on. Still, a well-placed crack to the head can knock anybody out, no matter how big you are or how often you go to the gym. A good boxer, even a golden glove out of the Windy City, will fall as hard as the laziest sack of shit you can think of. Hell, a single punch can kill a person if you know what you're doing. The human head doesn't take too kindly to being rattled about.

Daniel's childhood had been filled with bloody noses and wild fisticuffs, the kind of fights kids have, arms swinging all over the place, each boy too worked up to do any real damage. He'd get a bruise or a swollen eye. Mom would overreact. Dad would worry about it happening again, since dad likely went through the same thing. Parents, as a general observation, do not like seeing their children's blood. Most folks will try to hash things out with the parents of the offending party, which often leads to fights of their own. Others will enroll their precious little angels into the local boxing classes. The Lovings had been of the latter variety.

Earnest Ham was the first kid to do real damage to Danny. He had been a grade older than the incoming freshman and the boy's fathers hated each other. Herman Ham goaded his son into picking on the younger boy. Louis Loving warned Danny Loving to expect a hard time from the Ham kids and they did not disappoint. On the first day of freshman year, the right zygomatic bone in Danny's face was fractured by Earnest.

It was a sucker punch that had caught Danny off guard and when he leaned forward to catch his breath, Earnest cold-cocked him. Danny woke up in the emergency room. His jaw would be wired shut for the next ten weeks. Earnest broke two fingers, though since the altercation happened off school grounds and outside classroom hours, he faced no disciplinary actions from the school. My dad begged me not to do anything stupid in retaliation.

"It's Daniel's fight," he had said.

Louis Loving bemoaned the money wasted on boxing lessons and washed his hands of the whole thing. He was no fighter, himself. Ruth Loving's approach was both warmer and colder than her husband's. Danny told me that she kissed him goodnight and brushed his hair with her fingers for a long time. "I love you," she had said to him, "but you simply have to fight back. It doesn't even need to be a fair fight, really. Pummel him when he least expects it." That was her sage advice. "Go after him in the middle of class, in front of everyone," Ruth said, "even the teacher. Not right away, mind you. Wait till your teacher is in the middle of reading, or going over a lesson, and then casually go over to Earnest and hit him just as hard as you can. You'll get into trouble, but not with me. Not with your father. I promise you that. The world is full of people like Earnest. You'd better learn how to deal with them."

I admit to some amount of jealousy with regards to Ruth. My mother did not live long enough to give me such advice. Whatever maternal relationship I had was fostered vicariously through my friend and that luminous woman.

Danny braced himself against the bar. The attacker meant to have another go but Danny kicked the guy in the gut and sent the fellow ass over elbow. Danny leaned down and grabbed his attacker.

"Get up, you sonofabitch," he said.

I should have jumped up and put an end to it right then and there. But the moment got away from me. Truth be told, there was a small part of me that kind of wanted to see him hurt a little.

A loud snap echoed in the bar and Danny threw a hand out to his upper back. Shattered chunks of pool cue clattered to the floor. One of the other pool players stood beside Danny. Terrible idea, if you ask me.

Danny swept his second attacker's legs out from under him. The guy hit the floor hard enough that it winded him and he gasped and choked. Danny crushed that man's groin with an elbow, and then he bounced back to his feet.

Two of the pool players were down and out. But the other guy, the third party, he stood a couple of feet away and held his pool cue like a baseball bat. "You some kind of fucking cop?" the man barked. He lurched forward with quick jabs in an attempt to intimidate and jerked the pool cue as if he might swing at any second. Those boxing lessons came in handy for guys like this.

Danny studied the fellow's body language, looked that man up and down. He might swing that cue awful fierce but he definitely didn't look like he wanted to fight, and that was certain. Not that he really knew how to fight, seemed to me, and the way he held himself was purely defensive. He didn't want to get hurt. Nobody ever does. Fellow stood at about five-nine and weighed a buck-fifty at the most; dirty blond hair in a crew cut, wiry little arms defined more by malnutrition than by strength.

Danny took a step towards the guy. "I'm gonna make you eat that fucking cue," he said.

But Danny received a surprise blow to the back of his skull. He staggered for a moment, reached up and felt the back of his head. He looked at his hand and it was as bad as I feared. The palm was slick with red. Blood dripped to the floor and splattered amongst pieces of a shattered beer bottle. He glanced behind him at the offending party. The guy at the door had gotten off his stool and snuck up behind him, used Danny's own beer bottle to do the deed, which added insult to injury. The bartender wasn't too far behind and he had a baseball bat gripped in his right hand.

Shit, I thought.

Bartender pointed his bat at Danny and said, "You done started trouble in the wrong bar, Mac."

Danny steadied himself as best he could. "You know, I believe you're right," he said. "I'll just be seeing myself out—

Mister skinny-arms with the dirty blond hair creeped up and used his pool cue to put Danny in a choke hold. The guy that busted the bottle on his head reared up and punched Danny square in the gut. "Hold him up, Marvin," the guy said. "I'm a bust his face real good."

Not a one of them saw me stand up in the dark.

The bartender smacked his bat against one of the high-top tables and hollered. "Now you hold on a god damn minute." He marched up and shoved the eager pugilist backwards. "You done had your turn. I ain't played baseball in a long time." He tapped the end of the bat on the floor, twice. "You like baseball, Mac? I used to play when I was yer age, wasn't half bad. Not a lot of homeruns, but I always got a hit."

I figured I waited too long and Danny only had two ways out of this mess. One scenario saw him going to the morgue. The other scenario involved God Himself coming down from Heaven to lend a helping hand. Can't say I minded being his guardian angel. Made me feel like he needed me, even if a part of me knew I had a hand in his current predicament.

Then, the bartender hunkered down into a real hitter's stance. He spread his legs evenly and kept his weight balanced in his hips. He held the bat out to test the distance and rested it lightly on Danny's cheek. And then, he pulled back as if waiting for a pitch.

"Too high," Danny gurgled.

"What'd you say to me?" asked the bartender.

"Elbow's too high," said Danny. "Your back arm should be in the same plane as your rear shoulder. No wonder you didn't get any homeruns. You don't know what the fuck you're doing."

"You sack of shit," said the bartender. He spat on the floor and raised his bat like a club, like a caveman would.

Even though I carried the knife, I'd never had to use it, not once in my whole life. The blade looked as nice as the day I bought it. Thought that was about to change. My daddy told me everything changes when you kill a man, every little thing, even the taste of food. I didn't believe him at the time.

Danny closed his eyes. I came out of the shadows intent on putting my blade into any man that wanted it. But I didn't even get to raise my weapon.

Now, normally, when folks hear the loud report of a hand gun, it rightly fills a person with terror, but I daresay Danny flushed with relief, even if his ears rang like crazy. Mine certainly did. When he opened his eyes, I think he expected to see a cop or two standing at the entrance, like angels from on high. Maybe they'd flash badges and yell at everybody to get their hands up, like on the *teevee*. State he was in, I'm sure he hoped they'd radio in an ambulance. Danny had been worked over and looked like he meant to pass out.

Except, what he saw in front of him wasn't anything like that at all.

I had forgotten about the old lady and the bobcat. From the looks of things, everybody else forgot about her, too. The baseball bat sat on the floor. The slugger had a huge chunk taken out of it by the bullet she fired, which knocked it clean out of the bartender's hands. The old lady was a good shot and I thanked my lucky stars for that.

"You boys had your fun," she said, and motioned toward the back of the bar. "Now go on. Put those hands on the pool table where I can see them. I don't want to have to hurt you."

Smoky tendrils crept from the barrel of her gun and wrapped around the woman. She seemed to simmer and steam, like an angry spirit. Gunpowder smelled like Hell. The bobcat stood with its back arched high and screamed like a witch in a nightmare I had as a child.

Danny woke up in a white claw-foot tub. The old woman and I

had sat him upright, with his head rested against the rim. She filled the water up to his waist. May have started out warm but I figured it got plenty cold since, enough so that the sensation dragged him back into consciousness. Surely, Danny's body still hurt from the whipping, so I couldn't imagine he didn't appreciate the chill. His skull must have felt like it weighed a million pounds, the way he let it roll on his shoulders. Danny reached up and found a towel had been wrapped around his head. Finally, he noticed me on the toilet, sitting and watching him.

Not using it, just to be clear, only waiting for him to wake up.

"You sent that letter, didn't you?" Danny said.

I said, "How you figure that?"

"Mom's handwriting," Danny said, "isn't nearly as nice."

"But you came anyway" I said.

Danny shrugged his shoulders. "Figured you impersonating my mom meant something mighty important. To you, anyway." Danny groaned and shifted his weight in the tub, trying to move to his side. He faced the wall, his back to me.

My mind raced. I wanted to say so many things, too many things, and I felt like if I opened up, then everything would rush out in a flood and we'd drown. I opted for keeping my mouth shut. Let him do the talking if he wanted.

The bathroom itself appeared immaculate. Soft, recessed lighting above, no dust, no offending odors, you'd almost assume the room went unused. Bottles of shampoo and soap, each filled to varying degrees, were the only signs of life.

The tiled floor wasn't solid white, there was a hint of blue, and the grout was without stain, likely as gray as the day it was set. White wood trim lined the bottom half of the walls and stood as high as the tub was tall. From the top of the trim to the ceiling, everything was robin egg blue, a cool and tranquil color. A couple of framed black and white photos of flowers hung parallel to the door. I swear I could smell them, a perfume I couldn't quite place.

The room must have meant a lot to the woman if she kept it in the present state. Clean as a hospital ward, or, perhaps even more fitting, a sanctuary. The old lady had been nice enough to let us into her private getaway. I felt very much like an intruder.

The bathroom door opened, slowly. She poked her head in and smiled at me. Gave me a little wave, and then whispered. "Haven't seen so much blood since the war," she said. "But I've stitched up worse, believe me."

"I thank you, surely I do," I said. "I imagine you'll want us out of your hair directly."

Danny looked over his shoulder and said, "Who the hell are you, lady?"

"Surprised you don't remember me," she said.

Danny sat up, sloshing the water, and turned to face her. He stared her up and down, and then looked back and forth from the old woman to me, as if I could solve this puzzle for him. I shook my head.

"No, ma'am," Danny said. "I'm sorry. I don't have a clue."

"Eunice Smith," she said, "I taught English at the high school. Ernie Ham beat the holy hell out of you, if I recall. I never liked that boy, but you always seemed like a good kid. A smart kid. What the hell were you doing in Peterson's?"

"Getting my ass kicked," he said.

"Well, you certainly did a stand up job of that," Eunice said. "Shame your friend here didn't jump in any earlier. Imagine I'd have you both in my tub."

"Nicky's a lover, ma'am, not a fighter," Danny said and

laughed.

"Well, you should be grateful for him," Eunice said, as she stood next to me. "He limped your sorry butt to my car, not that you probably remember any of that, or the nonsense you talked while I drove the two of you back here. Passed out before we could get you in the tub. But we managed." She patted me on the shoulder.

Felt good to have someone in my corner.

Eunice snapped her fingers and pointed at Danny. "You go on and wash up now," she said. "There will be clothes on the bed in the room at the end of the hall. I took the liberty of throwing yours away since they were covered in blood and looked dreadful. I'll be waiting downstairs." She walked out and into the hallway.

"The money?" Daniel said.

"Don't you worry," Eunice said. "I'm no thief."

I winced.

Danny called out. "I didn't mean that!" But Eunice didn't respond. Danny cringed at his own remark and rested his forehead against his palm. I felt even more like an intruder than before.

"Hurry up," I said, and then got up and walked out.

The upstairs hallway was without a window. The only light present crept from the open doorway at the opposite end of the hall. A second door in the middle of the hallway had been shut. Guessed it to be the master and I let my fingertips brush against the door as I passed. I wondered if that room was as well-kept as the bathroom.

The open room faced east and soaked up the morning gloom. A pair of folded denim and a plain white button down sat on the foot of the bed, as promised. They were clean, for sure, but smelled as though they'd sat in a drawer for a long stretch, maybe years. I glanced around and sitting on top of the dresser sat a framed picture of a young man. A Purple Heart hung off the corner of the frame.

These had been the clothes of a son and this had been a son's room.

Bedrooms often told stories of those who slept within their quarters. Unlike the formality found in living rooms and parlors, a bedroom was home to more personal accents. Candid photos of lovers and friends, keepsakes and trinkets, it all served as commemoration for moments made memory, the kind of bittersweet affects that would cause the owner to pause and reflect.

This entire bedroom was a keepsake, but it didn't belong to the deceased son. I gathered this was Mrs. Smith's museum to a life snuffed out. I wondered if the bedroom was as it had been, or if the woman had arranged it just so. Perhaps the room was as her son left it, only tidied up a bit, as it seemed the woman was wont to do.

Everything was clean. Everything was ready. This room waited for a return that would never, ever happen. I stood in the center of a broken heart.

Mrs. Smith sat at her linoleum kitchen table. She read the morning paper with one hand and held a steaming mug of coffee in the other. Two more cups sat across the table and two chairs had been pulled back and obviously meant for Daniel and me. Neither of us could help but notice the gun which sat on the table by her elbow.

Danny motioned to the revolver. "I'm not some kind of criminal, if that's what you're thinking," he said. "I'm not wanted or anything."

She did not look away from her paper. "It had crossed my mind," she said.

"I'm trying to keep a low-profile," Danny said. "I mean, I was. I kind of mucked that up."

Mrs. Smith let the paper fold over and she looked at him. "I hear your daddy is in trouble," she said. Her eyes turned towards me and she added, "Among other things."

I nodded and said, "You heard right."

"And you think you're going to swoop into the desert"—she paused and smiled, looked down at her feet and shook her head—"and play the hero."

"Say it like that and it sounds silly," I said. "But, yeah, guess that's what I aim to do."

Eunice said, "You know, I hate to say it, and I hated hearing it for so many years." She rested a palm on the handle of the revolver. "But is there anything I can do to help?"

I considered the beating Danny took at the bar. He tried to take in a deep breath but his ribs hurt like hell. I could see it in the way he screwed up his mouth and squeezed his eyes shut. Odds were high we'd run into trouble of that sort again. I needed as much of my cash as I could keep, but parting with a little bit wasn't going to hurt.

The price of the gun was negotiated quickly and a little extra thrown on top for the woman's kindness. Eunice Smith wished us well and hoped the best for us both. Finally, she made mention of her son, and how Danny reminded her of him. She retrieved her son's leather bomber jacket from the living room closet and presented it to Danny. "It gets cold at night in the desert," she said. And, as it had been with her son, Eunice Smith would never again see Daniel Loving. He walked through the front door of her home and into forever.

The sun threatened to crest Hogback Mountain as Danny and I walked up to my car. Sunrise was an event I had always held in high esteem. Hardly anything more beautiful existed in the world than a sunrise on a clear day. It was unfortunate that it happened so early in the morning. I always fancied myself a night owl, fond of brunch but never breakfast. But Danny, he was worth the inconvenience of dawn.

"You're better off asking the police for help," Danny said. "Nothing good'll come of this. You have to know that. There are people that don't want me back in town. Rae's old man, most likely, is one of them. You have to understand something. I didn't leave town because I wanted to. I left town because I was asked to do so. Now, you seem to be a fine little detective, digging up clues, meeting me out here and forging notes. That's why I don't think you need me for this thing you're setting out to do. I don't need you piecing that mess together. I don't want to find out what you want to find out. It's not going to help you, and it sure as hell ain't gonna help me none. You think my dad's guilty and you came looking for a ghost to help you prove it."

I sprang in front of him. "I'm not looking for a ghost, goddamnit," I said. "I'm looking for my friend. I cannot do this without you."

Danny said, "I don't know what you want me to say."

"I don't need to hear a goddamned peep out of you," I said.

"Because you think I'm going to do the right thing," Danny said. "Is that it?"

"After you knocked up Rae, I watched you throw your whole life away because you thought it was the right thing to do. You left town, left everything and everyone behind, no questions asked," I said. "That's a hell of a resolve. I hate you for it. I surely do. And I miss you something fierce."

Danny said, "I didn't have anything to do with your dad getting killed."

"Never crossed my mind," I said.

"You asked me to come home, so I did," Danny said. "Simple as that."

"Louis is a suspect," I said.

"There can be more than one," Danny said. "Is he an official suspect, or is he just *your* suspect?"

"About a month or two ago," I said, "I get into this really weird conversation with a city clerk. I don't know him very well, but he's nice enough. As he's passing me on the sidewalk, he grins real big, asks if my dad is going to be looking for a new line of work. I shrug my shoulders. Not unless surveyors office goes out of business. To which he says, I don't know about out of business, but it looks like it may change hands real soon."

Danny said, "How would a city clerk know any of that?"

"Exactly what I asked him."

"Let me guess," Danny said. "He heard it through someone else."

I laughed. "Of course he heard it from somebody else," I said. "Living in Klamath is like playing a giant game of telephone."

"Friend or relative?" Danny said.

"Neither," I said. "His wife, turns out, she's a secretary at Noble & Sterling."

"I thought they did wills and estate stuff."

"They do indeed," I said. "But this wasn't about a will or anything like that. It was a contract, a sales contract, to be precise."

"And my father was the one asking for it," Danny said.

"Bet your ass he was," I said. "Didn't think squat about it at the time. The business never interested me, really, couldn't have cared. Always left that shit to the old man. But when the police found his body out in the desert, that weird conversation came roaring back to me."

Danny said, "You reckon he tried selling the business without your dad finding out?"

"I do not think your father was selling anything," I said. "Bet you he was trying to buy."

"Guess your dad wasn't selling," Danny said.

"That," I said, "is a helluva way to put it."

"And you," Danny said, "want my help finding the man."

"If he did it," I said.

"You think that will make everything square between you and me," Danny said. "Right?"

"I guess shit will never be square between us, Danny. But maybe you won't think we need to be enemies. Hell," I said, "you do this thing I'm asking and I might even try to forget you exist."

"Sounds alright by me," he said.

"Let's call it a deal, then." I held out my hand. "You and me are going to shake on it," I said, "like gentlemen."

And we shook.

Not a word passed between us during the whole drive out to Adel. We met with the two men I'd hired to help track Louis Loving. They claimed to know the desert like the back of their hand. They knew every coyote well. No trouble whipping up jackrabbit stew, either. Even claimed to have helped build a church out there, years ago, for a mad preacher who found himself gunned down.

We ate one last civilized meal in the town's lone diner. The hired hands talked amongst themselves, with both Danny and I interjecting on occasion, but never addressing each another. If the men noticed, then they kept it to themselves or didn't care. They'd get paid either way.

After dinner, those fellows took us to a livery stable at the edge of town and arranged for our transportation. Four horses, one for each of us. Dark crept across the sky by the time we hitched up and rode southbound into the desert.

When I looked up, I didn't see a single star in the sky.

Ed Best was running his trap but Ed was taller and wider and meaner than the rest of us so we let him.

The four of us were sitting around the campfire drinking whiskey to stay warm. Oregon desert is cold at night and dark and the stars never did come out, as if we wandered into some other reality, even though it was just the clouds. You couldn't see them, but it had to be the clouds. Ed and me and his buddy, Ezekiel—Zeke, we were told to call him—and the most sullen member of our little hunting party, Danny. We were all out here on the same job. But I guess we all had our own reasons for taking the work.

We had no ice but that didn't matter much since we had no cups either. The whiskey bottle moved clockwise, from man to man, except when it reached Ed. He'd take his sip and toss the bottle at Danny, even though Ed could just as easily have leaned over and handed it to the kid. About a quarter ways through the bottle our conversation crashed into the subject of God.

Ed thought God was just and kind and all things happened through His guidance whether or not we saw His hand. He said he spent three years in prison with only a bible to read. He told us that those three years behind bars were a revelation. He knew the

Truth, he said.

Zeke rolled his eyes and said miracles were bullshit and if God loved us so much he wouldn't spend so much time killing us or letting us kill each other. Zeke turned away from the fire and said, "You know my old man beat my mom to death? Beat her so her head swelled up like a balloon. Skin stretched out till it split and she didn't hardly have eyes to see, just two lumps of black and blue flesh. Can't look at a ripe plum without thinking of the old lady. Whole time he's beating her he's yelling at me to pray for her, and don't you know I did. Prayed for Him to save my momma and strike the old man dead. When she died he said I didn't pray hard enough. I haven't seen her since 1923, but my old man, that sonofabitch, lived another thirty years, and I never prayed a single time since." Zeke sat still and after a quiet moment or two he turned back towards the group. "What kind of a goddamned God does that to a little boy?"

Both Zeke and Ed were in their forties but looked much older, with hard lines in their faces and rough skin over their hands. Their lives shone through their eyes. Zeke's lifeless gaze only ever animated by anger. Ed was more like a spooked horse, brown islands lost in too much white, and they bulged as if each orb wished to escape his skull.

"Bullshit," Ed said. "You can't blame that on God any more than you can blame that on your poor momma. Man does what he does and sometimes what he does can't be reconciled."

"Maybe that's just some of His unseen handiwork you're so fond of," Zeke said. "Look, Ed, I get you're happy God found you in a hole and pulled you out of it. Don't mean I gotta be happy he shoved me in one and left me there. God watched my old man beat a saint to death. Don't give me that shit about all things through Him in one breath, and then deny it in the next. Don't do me that way." Zeke could speak this way to Ed because they were friends and shared secrets. Daniel and I would not dare.

Ed sipped from the bottle and then pitched the whisky at Danny. He spoke to us both but leaned towards Danny and stared him square in the face. "You know Zeke is lying through his teeth, don't you?" Ed motioned to the bottle, then pointed to Daniel and pantomimed drinking. Took Daniel a second, or maybe he didn't cotton to being told what to do, but he finally set to taking his turn, and Ed continued. "The man claims to believe in nothing, prays to no one, but you ought to hear him curse God all the same. Man don't believe in God ought not to curse him, don't you think?" Ed cocked his head towards Zeke and grinned like a baby who just shit their drawers.

"Aint you a right proper Christian," Zeke said. "Hold dominion over something that ain't yours to claim and deny a man his autonomy."

"Now you're just making up words to sound smart," Ed said. "I don't claim you, Zeke, but I know the Truth. Simple as that."

"I wish you'd talk about something else," Zeke said. He held out his hand and shook it at me and I gave him the whisky. "You get insufferable with that shit," he said. Zeke took a swig and ran his hand across his mouth, sucked through his gritted teeth. "What's the use in talking about something you can't really know no how?"

"Now you're just flashing your ignorance, see. All you got to do to know Him is pick up His book," Ed said. He swung towards us and pointed. "I suppose you two are familiar," he said. "Don't tell me I'm out here in the dark hunting murderers with nothing but a bunch of heathens."

"I believe everything that's in the bible and the things I can't understand I believe the most," I said, keeping as straight a face as possible, even after I heard Danny laugh a bit.

Ed stood up. "That supposed to be funny, wise ass? You best keep that Mark Twain shit to yourself."

"Josh Billings, actually. But you were close, Ed. Not that I fault you one bit. Fellow isn't exactly Virgil."

"I'm asking you two shitheels if you believe in God and one of you cracks jokes and the other laughs like a buffoon."

Daniel said, "I can't speak for anybody but myself, or about anyone but myself, but my momma taught me people believe all kinds of things, and every one of them think they're right and you're wrong. Maybe we're all wrong."

I nodded. "Hear, hear," I said. But Daniel didn't seem to notice. He said nothing more, but his eyes locked onto Ed, and finally Ed sat back down and grabbed the bottle from Zeke.

We looked like four castaways on a little island of flickering light. And there may not have been a star in the sky but there was still whisky in the bottle. Our meager campfire looked desperate, as if it were afraid to die, or like it held on just to keep us safe and warm, a dying parent, and the last source of illumination in the entire universe.

"My old man tried hanging himself," Zeke said. He held the bottle just below his mouth and stared off into the distance beyond Daniel and I. He stayed like that long enough that it spooked me, like I'd turn around and see Zeke's dad hanging in the darkness. "Broke his neck but didn't kill him. They took him down to Klamath Valley Hospital but didn't keep him long. He looked like—did you ever see the Frankenstein movie where Bela Lugosi played Igor? His neck was all wrong and he walked hunched over. Nerve damage caused him to smile all the time. And the sounds he'd make just breathing. Sweet. Jesus." Zeke finally took his drink.

"Sounds like he deserved it," Daniel said.

"God works in mysterious ways," Ed said.

I eyed the bottle as it passed from Zeke to Ed. Whisky sloshed back and forth in its glass prison, glowed like amber when the fire light hit it just so.

"God works mysterious, alright," Zeke said. "When He works at all. And my old man may have been rotten, but I don't know if he deserved any of what he got. It ain't normal for a man to live through all that."

"He deserved it," Ed said. "Hell, he earned it after what he did to your momma. And to you."

Zeke had the eyes of a man on the verge of tears. Whether he was actually that sad or just a drunk was anybody's guess. One got the sense Zeke knew all about pain, and maybe he was one of those types for whom pain was all he knew. Man crack a smile, it'd send him to the grave.

"God saw over him, birth to death, right?" Zeke asked Ed. "That's what you believe, isn't it? And no talking around it, you hear? I want a yes or a no, and that's it. You really are a friend, you can do me that favor."

"Live through what, exactly?" I said. "The hanging?"

Daniel shifted from the ground. He stood up and brushed the desert off his back end, then grabbed the whisky but never took his eyes off of Zeke. There was a story coming and he knew it. Boy was still young enough to be excited for stories, and I felt my affection grow for him.

"What did you mean by live through all that?" Daniel said.

"God didn't want the man," Ed said. "Devil didn't seem to want him none, either. Damn, Zeke, how many times your old man try to kill himself? Yes, that is what I said, times. Got to be so the man would have to be tied down at night. Kept me and Zeke here on our toes. We were thick as thieves by then. I'd done my time and wandered down here to find work on a ranch. Done some bronc riding as a youngster, some wrangling, so I figured I could work horses or help with cattle. I'll be dipped in shit if Zeke here didn't need help on the old man's ranch. This was after he'd hanged himself the first time, so his body was done bent and he always had that grin. If you couldn't see him directly, chances are you could hear him. And if he got excited his breathing would get shrill and watery. Got so I'd taken to calling him Tea Kettle, but Zeke didn't like that none so I stopped. I found him on his second go at a rope. Zeke gone into town. I was in the sty tending pigs. Couldn't see the old man but he was making his little noises, until he wasn't. I got curious and found him swinging in the barn, face all red, pissing his self and smiling. Well, I cut him down right quick and the names he called me. Shit, I'm blushing just thinking about it. He grabbed my knife and started to cry and he said, 'Kill me or I'll cut your throat in your sleep.' And the whole time, grinning up at me, tears rolling down his face. He was a spooky sonofabitch."

"I still don't think he deserved none of that pain," Zeke said. "And that weren't no yes or no answer."

"Guess he really wanted to die," Daniel said. "Was that it, or did he try again?"

Ed grunted out a laugh but Zeke only looked down at the ground.

Daniel used to do odd jobs around the surveyor's office. Our fathers co-owned the place, so that's how we came to know each other. We had an easy way with one another. He's several years my junior, so I played the part of big brother, which was difficult because I loved him something fierce. He had no idea and I had no intention of letting on for fear he'd never want to speak to me again. Damn fool, got that Klamath girl pregnant, so getting him out of town seemed like a good idea. And I find it no small irony that we are two lost boys looking for their fathers. I figured it might be our last time together before his life changes for good and I'm stuck watching him from a distant cage, till he goes in the ground. Or I do.

"Did he ever manage?" Daniel said.

"You're darn tootin' he managed," Ed said. "Took him two more goes at hanging and one time he even opened up an arm real good. I was there for that one. Zeke is hollerin' up in the house and I get upstairs and, well, he was thrashing about and blood was up the walls and all over the floor. I knocked him out and we hitched up and tore off for the country doc. Klamath being too far out and too expensive. Had to throw away my shirt and pants. So did Zeke. Old coot lost that arm. You imagine that? Bent up the way he was, that smile, and now him missing an arm. Telling you, if that weren't no punishment, I don't know what is. Still, even in that mangled shape, he finally managed."

Daniel whistled. "Well, damn, how'd he do it?" he asked.

"Ed would tell you all about it 'cept he weren't there that day," Zeke said. "The old man put a bullet in his chest. I didn't even try to stop him. Wasn't entirely sure he didn't want me to go with him."

"He was forever begging you to kill him," Ed said. "Even woke up one morning to him sitting at the foot of my bed, smiling at me and saying, 'Kill me, Ed. It won't be nothing for ya to kill me.' Still get chills thinking about that. Not ashamed to say I prayed for him to die."

"Another unanswered prayer," Zeke said. "Shit in one hand, pray in the other. Course, I guess he did finally manage, so maybe all your prayer finally did some good."

"I wouldn't call an old man shooting his self in the chest the answer to a prayer," Ed said. "God wouldn't answer a prayer like that even if that was exactly what I was praying for, which it wasn't. I only wanted a peaceful end, is all."

Ed stood up and passed the bottle to Daniel, who had taken to warming his hands on the campfire. The nature of the conversation seemed to take some of Ed's bluster out of him. Maybe this was just the calm before the storm. Felt like we'd never finish that damn bottle.

"May be that God don't care right from wrong," Zeke said. "Not like you and me. Maybe your prayer is what let the old man finally do himself in, like God had no reason to take him until someone else wanted him gone. I mean, hells bells, I hated the man but I didn't want him dead. He was the only kin I had. Maybe you killed him, Ed. You and God, together. People are always killing in the name of God. Maybe God killed my pa in the name of Ed?" Zeke said, and laughed.

"I don't much care for your sense of humor," Ed said. But the way he said it, quietly, and how he stood there looking at the ground, a part of Ed wondered about the power of prayer. You could see it.

And the stars were still gone. And we still had whisky. Our little hunt would wait for sunup and sobriety. While I wasn't exactly warming up to these hired hands, I was happy enough spending time with Daniel. It had already been a strange trip. Couldn't imagine it getting any stranger. My pop always said I didn't have much of an imagination, though. Rest his soul.

"Tell you what, if God don't exist then what's stopping me from getting up and beating the shit outta you right now?" Ed said. He sauntered around the fire, a dirty look for each of us. "Not got nothing smart to say to that, I guess."

Zeke stood up. Not quickly, just kind of rose to his feet like a man resigned to getting out of bed come morning. He kept his hands to his sides.

"You got no authority over me, you gutless turd," Zeke said.

"Put your hands up if you want to challenge me," Ed said.

Daniel whistled. "You got yourself a conscience, don't you, Ed?" he said. "I thought all decent folk ought to come armed with the same moral equipment, so to speak."

Ed took a step towards Daniel. "You saying I ain't decent?"

"I say no such thing," Daniel said. "You make that argument all by yourself."

Ed raised his fist. "Boy, it is taking everything I got not to knock you upside the head."

Daniel laughed and Ed screwed up his face, more confused than agitated, but he did lower his fists.

Daniel smiled. "The impartial spectator," he said. "That's what Adam Smith called it."

"I don't know who the fuck that is," Ed said.

"Just another man trying to save us from ourselves," Daniel said.

Ed blew a raspberry. "Yeah, well, somebody done come along and saved what need saving," he said.

"Sure," Daniel said. "And He's coming again, right?"

"First smart thing you said all night."

"Guess He messed up the first time?" Daniel said. "What kind of almighty god is that?"

Ed, hands out, made for Daniel, and I pulled my gun and cocked that hammer before Ed could take a second step. Just like that, Ed came to his senses. He sat down and mumbled an apology.

Zeke said, "Take a drink, Ed. May as well."

"Pulling a gun on an unarmed man," Ed said. "Not very Christian."

"Hired you two because you swore up and down you could track any man or animal out here," I said. "Don't bother much with sermons when they're free, sure as hell not paying you for one."

"What's this Louis Loving to you, anyhow?" Zeke said.

I looked to Daniel and he met my gaze and it dawned on me that the truth of the matter had yet to be said aloud. Not that I could blame Daniel.

"Louis Loving is the man that killed my father," I said. "Or so say the police."

Daniel looked away and wired his mouth up in a pained kind of embarrassment that was unbecoming of him. Age crept into his youth. He had to feel much older than his age. An absent father surely did not help.

I stood up and then walked away from the fire until I swam in the night and the crackling of wood was but a whisper to me. The dry earth crunched beneath my stride, the sound of sand scratched along the nighttime breeze. All that earth then settled like a sigh. I wondered if my father was buried or scattered. And I wondered about the parts that weren't found, the bits of him that never made it to his grave back in Klamath.

Sounds of camp were as rare as light as I walked further into the dark. The desert spoke only in a strange tongue of peculiar silence, not unlike the moments after a heavy snow, but missing the icy echo which accompanies that winter phenomena. The silence of the desert can swallow a man whole, scatter words like so much dust to be carried off on dry winds. Sound here is pulled taut and stretched thin until it is rendered madness. A man left too long in the desert will forget the sounds he once knew. Owls in the early bruised hours, the robins praising morning embers, a dove's spiritual at that time when shadows are shortest, all the beautiful music sung as blood lines the western horizon. In the absence of sound, man will hear what he wants, however mad the tenor may be. He becomes the song he hears in his mind. I wondered what kind of silence must have sung us into creation.

A hand came down on my shoulder and I knew who it was without looking. I think it must be that way when there is love. I could see Daniel in my heart. Like faith, I thought, and I laughed at that.

"Doubt anybody knows less about God than Ed," Daniel said. "I mean, damn, where did you find those two? Hell's bells, don't tell me. I don't want to know what crazy places you been hanging around. Can't spend my nights worrying about you."

"Ed likely knows as much about God as the next person," I said. "By which I mean he knows a whole lot of nothing. The hell any of us know about anything, Danny? We split an atom, so what? All we did was make a bomb and kill folks with it. Way I see it, that is all we ever been up to anyway, since man first stepped foot out of the cave. All fire ever did was help us kill each other at night. Tell me you know your daddy any better than Ed knows God. No, sir, you cannot. By all accounts, our fathers were best friends since they were little boys, but here my father's dead and the authorities think your daddy did him and a couple other folks. Breaks my goddamned heart. Can't believe this madness hasn't driven your poor mother crazy. I know it sounds awful, but I am glad my mother's done in the grave."

"By your reasoning, no one knows anybody," Daniel said. "I don't know you. You don't know me. Seems you want to find my daddy so you can find out you're right and I want to find him so you can see you're wrong. You stand out here in the dark judging Ed for what he claims to know but here you are doing the same damn thing. Hypocrisy is its own kind of violence. Don't much matter the source."

"Shit fire," I said. "Now you're just extrapolating. I never said he was a killer, just stating the same facts told to me that were told to you. I hope to hell he didn't do it. Pete's sake, I just hope we find him, is all."

Daniel walked around and stood in front of me so that his person was in silhouette and all around his body glowed the light of the fire, like he was an angel before me. A halo of gold. Wings made of flame.

Daniel said, "For all I know you could well be the death of me."

The way he said it cut through me to my very core and for a moment I lost all sense of time and place. And I struggled with my words.

"I would give my life for you," I said.

Daniel turned away. He walked back to the fire, preferring the company of strangers to my own. What love he may ever have had for me went with him.

I stood alone in the darkness.

Ed said, "I want you to know how come I ended up in prison, how come that bible meant the world to me. I know I come on strong and I can see yous' all distaste for my attitude. I ought maybe to apologize but I'll tell you this story and maybe you won't think I need to."

"You don't owe them two nothing," Zeke said. He looked at us. "No offense. Ed, you don't need to open that wound if you don't want. That boy over there sees you as a hired hand and that is that. You don't owe him your soul."

"It is not my soul," Ed said. "Just lucky to have it on loan."

"I am begging you," Zeke said. "Ain't nothing need be told. Don't do this to yourself. Not with all that drink in you."

"Wound is already open, Zeke." Ed laughed but it was a hollow mirth. "Wound like that don't ever close. Not ever."

Zeke looked at us and shook his head in disappointment. He worked at his lip a bit and his agitation infected me. Before I knew it, before Ed said a single word, I found myself anxiously tapping my heel in the dirt. Daniel sat with his arms crossed over his chest like a man braced for strong wind.

Zeke handed the whisky to Ed.

"I beat a man to death," Ed said. "I beat his ass to death with the hand holding this here bottle of whisky. Had to been June because I were locked up for Independence Day. Could make out the colored lights reflecting off the bottoms of faraway clouds. Sure as hell heard the explosions. I'd had my heart set to forgive, I swear it. But there were one moment I saw her face and all that forgiveness got drained out of me and I became a monster and I did what monsters do. Before I knew it, I stood in front of a judge, and then I was staring through bars wondering what fireworks looked like. You see me now and you'd never think I'd been a married man. Oh, but I was. Got married young, fell in love with a girl I met at a county fair. She said she loved horses and I learned to ride. She came to see and when I got good—damn good—she said she'd marry. Made me the happiest man on earth, I do say. I guess we did what lots of couples do. After getting hitched, I took a summer to make some extra money. Took that and what I'd won riding bronc and bought a plot and built a home. We had ourselves a little girl the next spring."

"You two did this," Zeke said. He pointed at Daniel and I like we were two mischievous kids in a classroom. "This pain is on you now. I can't say where it leads, but it ain't nowhere's good." Zeke clenched both his hands. "You can't know a man's pain unless you share it," he said. "A broken heart recognizes its own kin."

"Zeke and I, we got our differences," Ed said. "But we got our similarities, too. We hurt much alike, he and I."

Ed raised the bottle to Zeke. Zeke placed a hand to his chest and nodded. Both men smiled at one another.

"Zeke's not wrong," Ed said. "But that's why I agreed to this job in the first place. You two seem to have a shared pain and I don't mind helping you through it if I am able. Guess that is up to you, though, if you feel you are willing. Judging by your silence, I reckon you both want to hear me out. Or maybe you just like a story. That's fine, too."

Ed guzzled whisky. "I miss you something fierce," he said, looking up to the great nothing overhead. "My baby girl, she lived for five years. Wonderful years. Likely my best. She lived long enough for me to see who she would've become. Long enough to replace my heart and my entire world. A man—wealthy feller—he run her over in his fancy car. She got pulled up in his wheel well and when he hit the brakes the car sounded like it was screaming right along with my wife. I can still hear the harmony they made." Ed closed his eyes. "I hear it all the time," he said. "Her little eyes were wide open. Body all twisted. He face were upside down. Didn't kill her right off. I seen her eyes move. She watched us for a moment as we came running. I were afraid to touch her but I told her I loved her and she blinked once and that was it. Looking back, I suppose lots of things died right along with her."

Ed looked at us. He handed the bottle over to Daniel. "Cheers," he said. "Drink to my little girl. And you"—he pointed to me—"drink to the wife who left me. Zeke, I want you to drink to the man I was. Let's finish this damned bottle and go to bed. Not before, mind you, to the very last drop. I'll drink to the man I killed. And his poor woman, if there's any whisky left."

Zeke said, "L'chaim." And immediately, Zeke shot a look to Daniel and me, as if he'd committed some grievous error. Daniel said nothing, likely because he didn't cotton to religion much at all, so people's beliefs were their own, and no trespass against him.

I nodded. "To life," I said. And that seemed to settle Zeke a bit.

Ed laughed. He slapped his thigh and stared into the dark. I imagined he saw his wife and kid out there, floating next to Zeke's father. Ghosts likely enjoy a good campfire and story as much as the living. Ghosts probably have more need for it, being removed as they were.

"Zeke is a good man," Ed said. "I give him a bunch of grief even though we believe in damn near the same thing. Maybe if I could start over I'd be a Jew. Forget all about this New Testament.

An angry God might be easier to reconcile in light of this Nazi business. Maybe I'd have been more forgiving. Who's to say?"

"Ed thinks accepting Jesus excuses his actions," Zeke said.

"A single action ought not define a man and Jesus knew that," Ed said.

"Jesus wasn't but a man himself," Daniel said.

Ed wagged a finger. "Shame on you," he said.

Zeke said, "Make believe you were my kin, my tribe. Tell me what you did was kosher in the eyes of God. Maimonides believed a thousand guilty be acquitted than kill a single innocent. You cannot justify. Though, I do not judge you."

"Innocent is a rare word, indeed," Ed said. "That man run her over, of that he had no innocence. At the time, I absolved him, thinking there weren't no malice in his actions. An accident is just that, no matter how horrible. I were wrong. I do not think even he saw his own dark heart. Many do not. Is that not the way of most men? Year on, I ran into him in a pub. Bought that man a drink. He bought mine. We shared tears, gave each other condolences. He seemed pitiable enough. Until he got talking about his wife—his *barren* wife, as he called her—and he looked me in the eye and he said, 'I never wanted a kid.' And I decided, right then and there, that he would never have one. Weren't nothing he would ever have to worry about. I followed him out to his car. Same god damned car. Like going to her grave. And I caved that man's skull in," Ed said. "Man bought the bottle what killed him. Eyes bled. Brains poured out his ears when I left him. He'd never be any deader."

"The bible," Daniel said.

Ed side-eyed Daniel and barked out, "The what now?"

"Your bible," Daniel said. "I get how you ended up in the

clink but you said nothing about your bible."

"Yeah, suppose you're right," Ed said. "Guess I owe you. Not enough to see the wound, is it? Gotta get in there," he said. He waved a hand at Daniel. "Nah, I admire your attention to detail. I ain't got nothing but wounds anyhow. Suppose that's one generation's gift to the next. Wounds."

"Gift that keeps on giving," Daniel said.

I said, "Ed, I propose we wait and hear the rest of your story in the morning. We've been up far too long and tomorrow ought to be taxing enough without us getting no sleep and drinking as much as we have. I suspect the day to be long, and the desert is an adversary on a good day. Let's not tempt fate any longer, shall we? Surely this can wait for sunup. Hell, I'll fry up some bacon, first thing."

"Here I am, opening up my heart," Ed said, "and you expect me to just close it up and call it a night because you'd like some shut-eye. Goddamnit, Nicky, I guess you'd tell me to roll over and die if I were an inconvenience to you. You want me to leave you and your young friend here to while away in the dark? Far as I am concerned, you can just shut the fuck up and listen."

"I want to hear about the bible," Daniel said.

"I know you do," Ed said. "And if I were you I'd want to hear about it, too."

"I guess I'm a sucker for a good story," Daniel said.

Ed said, "We aren't so far removed from the cave, you and I."

Ed smiled at that, and it was an honest smile. Color came to him, even in the dim, orange light we shared. Slits for eyes as his cheeks rose. A row of good teeth shone in the firelight. Whatever animosity he had shown to Daniel was now gone. Couldn't blame the man. Daniel was easy to love.

Ed took another drink. He looked at the bottle, curiously, as if he had never seen this drink before. Strange, I thought, as I'd assumed it was his bottle. He counted silently on his fingers and even looked up into the night sky for a moment. Then, he passed it on with a smile of sorts.

"So, what about your bible?" Daniel said. "Finish the story. I'd like to go to bed, you know?"

Daniel no longer braced himself. Perhaps Ed's disarming tone leant familiarity which caused his guard to let down. Seemed a silent truce had sprung up between the two. Maybe they were both simply comfortable in their certainties. Show me two men more sure of themselves than an evangelical and an atheist. Such a person does not exist. I suppose their camaraderie should not have surprised me.

Ed watched as Daniel took his swig, and then as Daniel passed the bottle to me. I might have tried to pass on any further drinking had Ed not been burning holes right through me with those eyes of his. Looked at us as though he not only wanted us to drink, but needed to see us do so, though, at the moment, I only expected it was that he wished not to drink alone.

"What is on your mind, Ed?" I said.

"I just wonder how come I see things you can't," Ed said.

Zeke cocked his head and squinted at Ed.

Daniel said, "Well, get on with it, man. I don't think I could get drunker if I wanted. Tell me how you come to love a book."

"Boy, I swear," Ed said. "You joke, but something is mighty wrong." Ed looked at me. "Can't you see it? Don't you feel it none?"

"If you mean the whisky, hell yes I feel it," Daniel said.

Daniel and Ed held each other's steady gaze.

"Get on with it, Ed," Zeke said. "Let's be done."

Ed turned. His sight was like a grip on his friend.

Ed said, "Zeke, can you think of a world where I could love you as fierce as I loved my wife? My god, man, I'd carry you off and wouldn't never again think of all this pain I caused, what pain I endured. And I think that's what done separates us from Him. The love. Sometimes, I don't think He feels it at all. And that's how come he created us, so we could feel it for Him."

Zeke had an uneasy smile as his eyes darted from Ed to the two of us.

Daniel whistled. "You sure you want to tell this story at all?" he said. "Seems to me you been stringing us along."

"Fair enough," Ed said. "Suppose I'll start where I left off," he said. Ed looked again at the dark above us at spirits only he could see.

"I beat that man to death, and sometimes I wish I hadn't but sometimes I think it were for the best, like I were meant to, like he and I both needed punishing and we were sent to one another to deliver. Can't say I know what he done or I done to deserve what we got, but we got it sure enough. Maybe living is justification enough? Sometimes you have to start at the end and work your way backwards to make sense of the story. Ain't that the way of a good mystery? Sherlock Holmes comes in at the end and tells you how everything fits together. I think God is Sherlock Holmes but the mystery is our lives, and He came to make sense of the senseless. I stood in court and listened to that judge as he read out my sentence. I didn't cry, then, but when I got up to go, there were that man's wife. I thought maybe she'd whoop and holler me down, but no lie, she just reached out and hugged me and said she forgave me. She held me as tight as anyone ever has, and then I cried. I cried as if she were my own mother come to comfort me. No one said a thing. No one pulled us apart. Whole court was stunned to silence. My tears and her whispering words echoed off those walls and everyone in that room got to witness real judgment. She told me she'd visit as soon as she were able and she did. Weren't no one in the whole world I wanted to see more. I lost my own mother when I were but a young man. Spanish flu. Somehow, this felt like she come back to me. She come that first week and you can guess what she gave me. She said long as I were willing, she'd bring her own bible and we could read together. And we did. That whole stretch, we read to one another. Telling you all, that cell may well been a womb. I was born in there. State looked kindly upon me and my time with her and they decided I could be let out early. Only person I could think to tell about it were her, but damndest thing happened. She gone and killed herself at the man's grave. She got no stone of her own in the cemetery, so I been saving money here and there. That's how come I took this job. Give her a right proper headstone, saint as she were."

Ed looked at each of us, though I couldn't help but feel he looked through us to that very moment when she died. He stared, then, into the fire. The man shook his head and sighed.

"It's like someone took out all my insides and all that's left is a howling wind. It never stops, this wind, but goes and goes in a circle, like retribution is a punishment you carry forever," Ed said. He motioned around and said, "Just like this eternal blackness we're sitting in. Like this whisky that won't finish."

Zeke, Daniel, and I looked at Ed, each of us adorned with our own confounded expression.

"Truth is usually hard to see," Ed said. "You're just too

wrapped up in what's going on in your own life to notice."

We were all a little dumbfounded. I knew we got an end to his story, but it wasn't quite what any of us wanted or expected. Ed seemed to be trying to tell us something, that much felt certain. If this speech acted as a last-ditch effort to proselytize, then I am not sure he had any converts. I certainly felt as though he were deliberately leaving some detail out.

"Watch," Ed said to us. "Nicky, you pass the bottle to Zeke. Alright. Now, Zeke, go on and take a drink. Same as you been doing. No more, no less. Go ahead and give it here."

"You sure are acting funny," Zeke said. "What are you getting on about, anyways?"

Ed frowned and said, "Tsk, tsk." He shook his head. "Guess I am on about the same thing I always been on about."

"You talk a lot of nonsense," I said.

Ed said, "Some people need that nonsense."

He pointed to me and then to Daniel, but then he seemed to stare at his feet, as if he realized he may as well be pointing at himself. His hand dropped to his lap and he wore a frown, sad at first, but the way he furrowed his brow spoke of a deep concern. The lines drawn across his face reminded me of the maps my father would draw and hang on the walls of the surveyor's office. And like those maps, I did not understand the terrain before me.

"I think everybody ought to check the time," Ed said. "Go on, now. Check yer watches," he said, "I'll wait.

Daniel said, "I ain't got a time piece."

Zeke said, "What are you getting on about, Ed? You gonna start performing magic tricks for everybody? Can't dazzle us with brilliance so baffle us with your bullshit? Don't dig your hole any further, man. Let us go to bed."

"Going to bed ain't gonna help you none," Ed said. "You're already asleep. We are all asleep. Born sleeping."

"Boys, I apologize," Zeke said. "Ed is always preaching. You know how some folks are. Using their own tragedies against you. It always ends the same way," he said, "repent or else you'll be damned to Hell. Well, I've been hearing it for years, if it's any consolation. He's just drunk and getting spooky, is all. How could he not be, all that drink in him? Nobody is gonna fault you boys none for rolling over and getting some shut-eye."

"I'm not drunk," Ed said. "And neither are you. Neither these two young men, either. Go on, wave a hand in front of your face. Get up and dance in a circle."

Zeke said, "Shit on you, Ed."

Ed placed a finger to his lips. "Shh," he said, and then he pointed to the black sky. "I done asked you to check the time."

"I got three," I said. But I looked at it, shook it, and held it up to my ear. "Damn, I guess it's busted," I said.

"Of course it is," Ed said. "Here, check mine."

Ed tossed his wristwatch to me.

I caught the watch and looked at the face, and then felt my stomach drop a little. "Three," I said. "And this one is busted, too."

Ed nodded sagely and said, "Now, Daniel here ain't got no time piece but I know Zeke does. Zeke, how about you pull out yer daddy's pocket watch and tell me the time you got."

Zeke reached into his coat to some unseen pocket in which I presumed he hid his father's watch, but what he pulled out was a gun, instead. There he was, working at that lower lip again. He kept the piece in his lap.

Zeke said, "I don't think I am gonna do that, Ed. And as a matter of fact, I am gonna ask you just as polite as I can that you go to sleep now. No need scaring these boys any longer with your crazy talk. Just roll over and close those eyes and I will wake you when it's light."

Ed stood up. He took his time. Guessed he must not exactly desire getting shot by his friend, or whatever Zeke was to the man, directly. He breathed as deep I ever seen a man breathe. Stuck his chest out. Kept his shoulders back. Seemed, though, Ed aimed to die with pride if it came to it.

"I don't need to see your daddy's watch to know what time it reads. Same as mine," Ed said. "Same as his." Ed jerked a thumb at me. "Be the same as Daniel's, if'n he had one."

"I don't aim to give you the satisfaction," Zeke said.

"That is fine by me," Ed said. He held up both hands. "I do not need to face your fear. That is on you and you will cross that bridge when it comes."

I said, "What in tarnation are you getting at, Ed?"

"I know what it means," Daniel said. "Don't need no time piece, either. Thought about it myself but figured I was too drunk to be making much sense. You're right, though, Ed. I ain't drunk at all," he said. "I reckon Ed is talking about the dark."

I looked around us. "Dark is dark," I said, "so what?"

"I'll show you so what," Ed said.

But Ed said nothing about the dark or the time or about God. He didn't say a single word. Ed held out that bottle of whisky and looked, again, at each of us, as if to make sure he had our attention. Then, he turned the bottle upside down. The liquor splashed against the thirsty earth.

Ed smiled. "Bottle never ends," he said. "Just like this

darkness, it just goes on forever."

Whisky poured and poured. The sweet-smelling spirit spilled into a puddle which fanned out in an ever-widening circle, until Ed's feet had been baptized. Daniel laughed, the nervous laughter of one who feared what transpired before his very eyes.

"Sun should've been up at least two hours ago," Ed said.

"That don't mean nothing," Zeke said. He stood up, eyes wide, mouth pulled back and showing off bad teeth. He raised the gun, pulled back the hammer, and yelled, "You make it stop, you hear? Or I swear I'll put a bullet in you."

I heard the stillness of the desert creep over the crackling fire. I heard the blood rush through my veins, heard that same rush through Daniel's, and the two men who dared each other to accept one another's reality. Each of us a rush of wind, becoming a maelstrom.

How long had it been dark?

Where were the stars?

Screams blossomed in the distant dark. Blood-curdling. Each of us turned towards the sound. Screams like a distant revival, like music.

Each of us stood frozen except Ed, who grabbed a protruding piece of firewood and wielded it like a torch. The man neither waited nor gave direction. He ran towards the terror.

Not to be outdone by his friend, Zeke grabbed his own torch and raced after Ed.

"Jesus H. Christ," Daniel said, hardly more than a whisper. He, too, took up a torch and went into the night. Only I went without fire. No need, as I followed the only three stars along the horizon.

The screaming most certainly belonged to a man . . . and something else I could not quite place in the moment. They were animal sounds, I guessed, high and shrill, but of an anger. This harmony vocalized a struggle, such an awful struggle.

For one moment, in that darkness, I thought I spied a ghost run past me in the dark. A wisp of a man whose terrified face looked all the world like Daniel's father, but he vanished as he passed and I reckoned him an apparition brought on by distress, terror, and too much drink. And I ran and ran after the three stars in the distance.

Screams raged.

One of the stars stood idle. In my temerity and terror I approached without caution. The star revealed itself to be Daniel, and in the distance, close to the other two stars, rang out a constellation of shrieks both man and animal, two tongues fused in a language of pain. I grabbed Daniel by the collar and drew him close but his eyes refused to meet my own. His vision locked on to the unseen and his mind conjured sights that supplanted the reality before him. He would neither advance nor retreat and I left him for the other two points of light.

I pulled out my gun and held it before me, like some ancient knight entering a joust.

Ed and Zeke stood far enough apart so that their torches flooded the scene like amber spotlights. They were the only stars whose light shone on this part of endless Hell. I moved through space like an unseen satellite, a pallid moon unencumbered by illumination, a silent witness to the demons which thrashed before the dull eyes of a terrified universe.

Four of these demons yielded flesh as black as night, skin pinned tight over muscle and bone, the famished nature which expressed itself through ribs and knotted joints quite visible in the yellow tenebrosity. They were, I thought, horses—foals, perhaps—but their mad tenor belied their stature. Beasts of burden, I realized, hopped and kicked and bellowed their song, which could be mistaken for no other. Feral ass, practically carbonized, colored as though each were forgotten in some inferno and left to cinder, now free to burn where they pleased. Each animal incandesced among those stretches of hide where blood ran and splattered their jagged frames. Blood worn on haunches and blood draped on withers. Their collective eyes glittered and shone like great black marbles.

A fifth demon looked very much a man. His clothes hung in tatters, flayed by gnashing teeth, and his exposed skin glossed with black blood. Whether the ichor belonged to him alone was anyone's guess, for as they tore at him and bit, the man gave back to them in return. Somehow, to my eyes, he was more feral than the menagerie which surrounded him.

One of the animals bore a hatchet that had been buried in the withers. The man leapt to the animal's back. He seized the handle and withdrew the blade. And then the man rolled beneath the creature and hacked into the inside of its thigh. The donkey reared up and arterial spray hit me in the mouth. When the beast fell over, the others erupted in screams and one even sounded as though it cried out, "No!" But it must have been a trick of my impassioned state of mind.

They bit at the man's flesh and he swung at them. When they retreated from his lacerating blows, the man turned to the fallen member and split open the donkey's belly, cock to sternum. Pitiful remains poured forth in a torrent of gore. White bone rose like ice from the ocean of viscous fluid. Human bones, some of which surely belonged to a child, floated amongst the effluvia. Shards of a skull caught my attention. My imagination draped the bone in familiar flesh, gave it eyes that looked not unlike my own. I fell to my knees before the skeletal gaze of my late father. This demon had been his killer and his grave.

The man, now nude save the black blood running head to toe, brought the hatchet down. Again and again he hacked at the sinewy neck and crushed bone, until the head loosed itself and what ran through a demon's veins poured from the ragged stump to be drunk by the hungry earth.

The other donkeys screamed in the distance, but no longer in anger. They screamed in pain. The anguish of loss tore through the pitch.

The man, exhausted by his brutal triumph, collapsed.

Ed handed me his torch. He picked up the man, put him over his shoulder, and carried the fellow all the way back to camp like that. I carried my father's skull in a kerchief, cradled the remains like a football. Danny, I reckon, carried nothing but his own torch. We did not pass him in the dark. By the time we made it to camp, there he sat by the fire. He never once looked up as we approached.

Zeke stayed behind with the carnage and for a few minutes the distance seemingly snuffed out his torch. Then a pinprick of light grew and grew until the man slipped from the darkness and into the glow of our campfire. He carried the donkey's severed head in his free hand. Like the whisky bottle, its contents yet poured forth.

"What you bring that awful thing back for?" Ed said. "Leave it be."

"Didn't think you would believe me," Zeke said. He dropped his torch and held the head up. "Thought I heard a whisper, but then I got close and heard him talking."

Ed shot a look in my direction. "He's spooked is all," he said. "Don't listen to him."

"It's not me you have to listen to," Zeke said, and then he tossed the severed head into the fire. Sparks issued from all sides. Flesh and hair sizzled. The rank odor hurt to breathe and stung the eyes.

Ed yelled, "Have you lost your mind?" He swatted at a burning ember that graced the sleeve of his coat.

Zeke raised an arm slow and pointed and spoke in a drawn-out hush, "Look."

The head quivered in the fire and the eyes fluttered, then shot open. Those black marbles rolled in their sockets and the thing looked at each of us. Muscles in the jaw flexed and the mouth widened. Black sludge rolled over the tongue and past the teeth to settle and sizzle in the flames. And when it spoke, its voice sounded like a man's and woman's simultaneously, and as though the voices were trapped in the deepest well. All the hair on my arms and legs tingled and my stomach sank and my heart beat against its cage like a distraught prisoner. Zeke clasped his hands together and openly wept. Ed crossed himself. Danny never moved.

"You will be lost to time," it whispered. "This planet is an unmarked grave floating through a black sea and lit only by a distant torch." The donkey's eyes bubbled over, running out of the sockets and into its mouth. "Pray if you must, supplicate. Scream into the casual void that swallows all life and light. All answers are the same."

Shrill and mad laughter burst from Zeke who now rocked back and forth on his knees. Ed marched over and struck Zeke across the face with an open palm and yelled, "Shut up, damn you." Ed looked at us and saw the blank expression on Danny's face so he pointed to me. "Get my shotgun," he said.

I scrambled past Danny and into the edges of frayed light where the horses had been staked, but I found only the stakes. I tried to speak. Fear choked me and tears welled in my eyes. I bit my hand to get ahold of myself.

"Horses are gone," I said.

Ed stuck his chin out and he wore a righteous angry frown. Veins throbbed at his temples. He rolled his wide eyes over me and Danny and then he hauled off to where I just come from. I couldn't see him, but I could hear him kicking and feeling around in the dark. "Goddamnit," he yelled. And he stormed back into camp with one of those long metal stakes gripped in his hands. He made way for the fire.

The donkey saw Ed coming and it screamed like I never heard in all my life. Not even in my worst nightmares. Zeke shot up off the ground with hands over his ears and he ran away. Ed brought down the spike like a hammer. The donkey's skull caved in on the second strike and pink matter belched from the open wound, but it kept talking.

"You'll die alone," it said.

The charred thing slid from its pyre to the ground and smoke billowed from its hollow eyes and its mouth and Ed kicked it back into the flames. No more words uttered, but it popped and sizzled and smelled like sulfur. The skin split and pulled away and revealed bones the color and texture of coal. Thick smoke rolled off the fire and did not rise in a plume but fanned out over the desert like a black fog until the ground was as dark as the sky and we could not see our own feet.

"Where are the stars?" I said.

"Shut your fucking mouth," Ed said. He kneeled down to check the unconscious man's pulse. "I think he's dead," he said. "Or damn close to it. Done what we could." Ed looked at me but pointed to Danny. "Get him on his feet," he said. "We're going after Zeke."

I shook my head. "That's suicide," I said.

"It'll be murder if we don't," Ed said. "Now get him up and let's go."

"I won't do it," I said. I held out an arm to Danny. "He can't," I said. "Look at him."

"He's fine right where he is." Ed said. "Fire's good company."

"I won't leave him," I said.

Ed cracked his knuckles. "I'm not asking you," he said. "I'm telling you. Leave him and let's go." He took a step, but stopped.

I pulled my gun and pointed it at Ed.

Ed laughed. "You gonna shoot me, huh? Tell you what, you little shit, you better kill me with the first shot 'cause I'll snatch that gun outta your hand and beat you to death with it," he said. Ed took a deep breath. "Now let's go get Zeke." He stuck his chest out and kept his shoulders back like he did before and I shot him in the head.

The darkness of the open desert swallowed up the pistol's report.

Ed's head whipped back and blood sprayed out his nose. He took two janky steps backward. Man tried moving his arms but his body would not cooperate. He stumbled for a second and opened his mouth like he had something to say, but there was only more of that black blood. His front bathed in the thick lacquer. Ed didn't fall so much as crumble. His last breath hissed like a popped tire. The fog rolled around him as his body shuddered its last and he looked like a night swimmer relaxed in a black lake.

"What did you do?" Danny said. He must have snapped to because now he stood upright and by my side. I didn't notice, preoccupied as I had been.

"It was a mistake,' I said, "helping you leave Klamath. And it was a mistake bringing you back."

"You shot him," Danny said.

"He meant for you to die," I said. "I wouldn't have that."

Danny said, "Zeke is out there somewhere."

"You and I are heading towards Adel," I said. "If that man still has his wits about him, then that's where he's heading. Sunup can't be that far off."

"What about that man we found?" Danny said. "We can't just leave him here."

"Can't take him, either," I said. "Not where he's going."

Danny crossed over and knelt down. He placed a hand on the man's chest and tried appealing to me. "He's breathing fine," he said. Danny placed two fingers along the fellow's neck just under the jaw. "Heart's beating like a drum," he said. "Ed lied to you. He meant to leave him, too, I guess. Why he bother bringing him back at all?"

"Ed fancied himself a man of morals all the way to the end," I said. "But the heart wants what it wants. Force him to pick between you all and Zeke, well, morals be damned."

Danny stood up. "Maybe this guy wakes up," he said.

"Maybe he don't ever," I said.

"Sun's got to rise soon," Danny argued. "You said it yourself."

"Bit of light won't keep you safe."

"Suppose you will."

"Told you I'd die for you."

"Heart wants what it wants, right?"

"I never once in my life put on airs," I said. "You know how I feel."

Danny got down on his knees and put an arm under the man. He gripped a limp arm and put it around his neck, then stood that man up. He staggered his breath and said, "Lead the way."

"You're a damn fool," I said. I shoved the gun into the waist of my denim then walked over. I took the other limp arm and put it over my shoulder. "On the count of three," I said.

"One."

"Two."

"Three."

We walked like that for some time. Heard nothing and saw less. Stumbled once but caught ourselves right quick and went on, not a complaint out of either of us, not a word. Not a star in the sky. No sun on the horizon. I hoped beyond hope that we were actually heading towards Adel and not further into the abyss.

Our eyes adjusted to the dark as much as they were able. We found that there were sights to see, as long as we were right on top of whatever it was we were seeing. That's how both of us came to a dead stop before crashing into a large boulder. Huge slab of rock had to be the size of a small house. Looked for the life of me like it had landed there, and maybe it had. Place had been nothing but volcanoes throwing fire and brimstone around long before man or animal lived and died here. We whispered to each other.

"I'll be damned," I said. "Think we could get to the top?"

"We could wait out this dark up there," Danny said.

I gave a low whistle. "Well," I said in my best drawl, "no shit."

Danny said, "How you figure on getting him up there?"

"I don't figure," I said, and I would have said more if not for the terror I felt.

A snap of a dry twig issued from the distance. If we had not stopped and weren't already whispering then we wouldn't have heard a damn thing, which I figured had to be on purpose. We had a mystery guest bringing up the rear. Three guests if I were a betting man. And there was something else, something closer, like pebbles ground underfoot. Loose rock dribbled onto my shoulders from above and I looked up. A figure rose in the dark and stood atop the massive rock before us. Whether friend or foe we could not yet know, until the figure spoke.

"Ed," Zeke said from up there. "Is that you?"

Zeke was alone, but I knew him armed, which meant dangerous. I gripped Danny's shoulder as tight as I could. "He went looking for you," I said, before Danny could admit to anything that'd see us come to a violent end. "Help us up, will you?"

"Us?" Zeke said.

"Danny's with me," I said. "And the feller we found."

"He awake?"

"We carried him the whole way."

"God damn," Zeke said. "Could have left him, you know, state he was in."

"Help us up, man," I said. "There's something out there."

"I know it," he said. "Heard them beasts clomping around earlier. Think they were trying to suss out how to get me, but they don't climb none, so here I sit."

We didn't say anything in return. Zeke squatted down and reached out a hand. Danny went up first. Then he and Zeke dragged up the unconscious fellow. Only Danny helped me up. Zeke sat damn near like a dog at the edge of the rock. His eyes were as wide as they could go, as if looking like that might help him see any better. Then he turned his ear out and I understood. Zeke listened.

We all listened.

"Three of you breathe too damn loud," Zeke said.

He didn't have to ask. Danny held his breath and so did I. Nothing much to do about the passed out fellow, but he seemed to rest easy.

The three feral asses posted themselves in the distance straight across from where we perched. You could hear them even though they walked with a light step. Unintelligible whispers seemed to ride the silence. Never in my life would I entertain the idea that they talked to one another, but I could not deny what I saw with my own eyes at the camp. These bastards plotted our doom, but the thin chatter ceased and their gait seemed to fan out. They were moving away from one another and around the rock in three points. Nothing more for a minute or two until a grunt sounded directly ahead. Those savage beasts began to close in. Without a thought in my head I drew my weapon.

"I got five bullets left," I said. "How about you?"

"Not got but what's in my gun," Zeke said. "Wasn't exactly counting on . . . whatever it is that's happening."

The desert spoke to us three in its strange tongue of peculiar silence. Shallow breath interrupted occasionally by the snap and smash of dry sage and brush. Sometimes these sounds came from the left and sometimes from the right, but never from the front, and I wondered if that bad beast waited and watched like a commander. We three imagined sounds when there was an absence of sound and with those phantom sounds came phantoms themselves. In our desperation to understand and know these creatures we conjured spirits in the distant dark. We saw what we wanted and kept those visions to ourselves. Zeke's dead father hanged above us and he stared at me and smiled and put a finger to his lips and shushed me. The rope cinched around his neck stretched up and up into the infinite night, to where I cannot say.

In this silence we sung all manner of atrocity into creation and in that way we were as God must be. Mad and alone and dreaming in the void. We become the songs we hear in our minds. Heaven is a desert you cannot see but for the phantoms you give life. They are in your image.

God is insane.

The sun remained hidden. An hour passed since we last heard those brutes trampling parched earth. Got so we felt like talking again as a way to pass the time and Zeke told what he knew of the area and the animals.

"Used to be a big operation out here called for hauling borax," Zeke said. "Mostly by jerk line, mule power, but they had donkeys too. Lots of mining companies did back then. But the rails saw an end to that when I was still a young man. Well before your time. Borax mine shut down. Sold off what they could. Lots of animals were just let loose. Most died, but some kept on in pockets," he said. "Find food where you can in the desert."

If Zeke knew anything more then he decided to keep it to himself. Nobody spoke. My mind circled back to the earlier conversation. I'd poked fun at Ed, but present conditions forced me to reconsider the totality of my beliefs.

"It is odd," I said, "the internal and gnawing suspicion that you are an imposter in your own skin. I don't belong here, I think. But then again, I don't think anyone belongs here. I think all this .

. . life, I guess you'd call it, is really nothing more than a vacation. We're taking a break from an endless nothing. A womb and a grave—though not mutually exclusive—are really nothing more than a terminus. Where are you going? Where have you been? Did you have fun pretending to be a human being with a name and a job? Did you hear Love and did Love call to you?" I said. "You know, of course, what that is, don't you? Love is tapping out. Love is the void, beckoning your return. You've had your vacation, imposter, it's time to let someone else pretend for a while.

"And you dream. Sometimes, dreams are filled with people, some of them you recognize, some of them you don't, but there are always people. In almost every dream," I said, "maybe it's only one other person or maybe it's a whole roomful of people. When your dream ends, do you ever wonder where they go? They aren't you, right? It's not like they're acting under your purview. What happens when the dream is over, I think that's what God is. I think God dreamed us into reality and He wants to see if we can do the same thing for Him. I don't think He can exist here unless we make it possible. In science fiction stories, the scientists are always looking for holes in space and little slips in time or gateways to other dimensions. What if we never had to go looking for any of that? What if we are the gateway? We were made in God's image and then we created all manner of things in our image. Maybe that is the way God comes here. Maybe all this toil and hardship is really just God slowly making His way through the gateway.

"You ever hear folks say that their work is a compulsion? It is not, no sir. It is an order. We are programmed to work and to create. We were programmed to create since the beginning. Don't you see? Creation begets creation. All these facsimiles, bearing children, building homes, painting, sculpting, writing, busting apart atoms to win wars . . . one way or another, all creation leads to God. One cannot simply walk into reality. We dream. Our dreams inspire. We create lives from these dreams. We inspire others. We create children, and we give them our dreams and our work and they pick up where we left off. It has always been that way. Love is nothing more than a piece of programming meant to keep us going. To keep us creating." I sighed, quite satisfied with myself, and said, "It's all for Him."

Zeke's riotous laughter caused me to jump and then he said, "Nobody is as important as a man at his own funeral." He laughed again but calmed himself and cleared his throat. "If you must feel sorry for yourself," he said, "at least make it short."

"You go to Hell," I said.

"My boy," Zeke said, "we are already there."

More laughter cracked through the dark, but of a humor altogether meaner and knowing and not of man. I'd once heard claim that all creatures were capable of laughter. How nice to know that fact extended to demons. It felt strange to consider laughter in a place like Hell. Though I had once been reprimanded for laughing during a Christmas service. Inappropriate was what my father had levied at me, but he should have said what he meant. I sinned in my merriment. Maybe Zeke was right.

Danny said, "I just remembered something wild." Rock scraped from behind as Danny shifted his weight. "Not even sure it's worth sharing," he said, as he crawled closer to Zeke and me. Danny patted my shoulder.

"Remember my mother said she knew a man who believed that God's face was black as night," Danny said. "That he thought the shadows were God's eyes watching over us."

The unconscious man drew a sharp breath. I feared him having an attack of some kind or another. None of us were capable of much more in the way of medicine than sitting bedside and witnessing last rites. But then he sat bolt upright as if he'd been startled from nothing more serious than a nap.

"Your mother's name is Ruth," he said.

And the dried blood seemed to glow on his skin because the dawn had finally come.

"Who are you?" Danny said.

I stood and held out my hands as if I could will the light to me. I felt like an abandoned child reunited with family. The morning gloom promised loving embrace. I reached for the light in the east and I cried.

"Your father's name is Louis."

I looked above to the faded luminance of retreating stars. I covered my mouth in an act of repressed joy. I pointed to the sky. "Look," I said. "It's a miracle." And I turned to my companions but they looked neither to sun nor stars, but at this creature clothed in blood.

"I am the indifferent teeth which rends you to pieces," he said, "the jaw that grinds your bones to dust. Ruth delivered you to me and, before you die, you will deliver me to Ruth."

I placed myself in front of Danny. Zeke stood in front of me. The man smiled at us as I had smiled at the sun and I felt terrified.

"My sermon is blood," the man said. "My benediction is death."

Zeke raised his pistol.

"I have killed so many," the man said and pointed at us, "but only you will die a dozen deaths with me in the dark."

Zeke fired off a round. A blossom opened up in the man's

cheek the color of deep red. The color ran down his face and dripped off his chin to his chest and the rock below. The man bared his teeth like an animal.

Ed had told us he had punishment coming and that he and the man who killed his daughter were sent to one another to deliver. Ed claimed not to know what trespass he had committed to deserve the death of his little girl but that he got it all the same. But I knew what I'd done to deserve this man's wrath. I made of myself a murderer. And now the howling winds of retribution circled within me. I feared death and this man most of all.

"Run," Zeke said.

And we did.

Not sure how many minutes passed before I realized I ran alone. Danny had jumped down from the rock ledge same as me, but somewhere between hitting the ground and taking off, we lost one another. Zeke fired off two more shots in quick succession. I almost stopped running right then and there, but all of a sudden, Zeke screamed and the sounds he made were unnatural and pitched high. Another shot fired off, but the screaming didn't stop, so neither did I. Could have run forever after that.

And then sounds like the distant thunder of three separate storms gathered behind me. Didn't have to look because I knew what was coming. Figured I had a minute before they overtook me. Five bullets were all the currency that remained with which I might purchase a little extra life. Their punishment could be me, but only if I were a deadeye.

I spun around and took a knee. Aimed. Fired.

I couldn't hit the broadside of a barn and they kept roaring across the expanse.

Aim.

Fire.

Sonofabitch.

I only had but three shots left and I missed two more times so I put the gun in my mouth. No way in hell I'd miss this one. Felt awful sorry for myself. They got damn close and I shut my eyes real hard but I went on living and the thunder halted. I cracked open one eye and then the other. Took the gun barrel out of my mouth and stood up.

Two of the donkeys stood on either side of the third that lay in a heap on the ground. They nudged the body but their friend did not respond. There was a faraway report what sounded like the crack of a baseball bat and, about a second later, one of the standing donkeys jerked its head to the side and fell over dead.

That last donkey looked in my direction and brayed and then bolted westward away from the rising sun. Reduced by all that transpired and from such a close brush with death, I let the pistol fall to my side and I sat on the dust and watched and waited for my savior. A figure approached from the south and waved. It was Danny.

I attempted a wave of my own but weak as I was I only raised my hand and let it fall back to my lap. I smiled at the thought of reunion but the smile did not last. This was not Danny, but he wore Danny's clothes. I raised my pistol.

He called out my name and said, "You know who that bullet is meant for."

"You killed him," I said, not without struggle. "Killed both of them."

"They're waiting for you," he said, and pointed to the south. "They're back at the rock. You can join them if you want," he said, and he offered his hand to me. "It's what He would want."

I put away my pistol and the man lifted me to my feet as though I weighed but a feather.

"Do you think God is good?" I said.

"No," he said. "Nor is He evil. Nihil is bereft of all morals, transcendent and passed through the Gates into Immaculate Void. Morality is just another punishment for the damned," he said, "another trick bestowed upon us by the Deceiver. Flesh is a cell and life a sentence."

I said, "Are you going to kill me?"

He smiled. "I don't have to," he said with a nod. "Do I?"

The man left me and walked on and I watched until the desert distorted his frame and swallowed him whole. The rock was much further than I had anticipated. Zeke remained stationed where I'd last seen him, though I could not find his head or right hand. Danny lay face down in the distance with his arms and legs twisted at unnatural angles. I did not dare to go any closer for Danny was now as far away from me as it was possible for a human being to go.

What love he may ever have had for me went with him.

I was alone.

Each one of those men got a proper headstone. I made sure of that. A good man ought to have every intention of paying back what is owed. Ed and Zeke and Danny were three lives forfeit on my account.

"Every epitaph I write is a story," Earnest Hamm said, "for the best parts of us that live on forever." And he just beamed. Probably practiced that shit in front of a mirror.

There was a lot of shame inherent to a place like Hamm

Monument Company. Not so much from the people that worked within because good sales people are shameless, but it was palpable coming off visitors. Spending small fortunes on rocks for a person who will never see the damn thing felt like a strange kind of extortion.

But I knew where my grave would be. I had seen the headstone. It said nothing aside from my given name, the year of my birth, and the year of my death, separated by a cross. A strange request, Earnest Hamm had said. I lied and said that a cancer was eating my insides. He apologized. And the stone was made to order, simple, formal, and cheap, not unlike the people who would surely oversee its fabrication.

The funeral, if there was one, would be small. Immediate family, I imagined, with none of the extended showing up, which was only fair. I wouldn't go to their funerals, either.

To what did I owe those dusty devils whose beliefs fall utterly short of reality?

Nothing.

The hour was still early, and I figured Danny's mother yet slept. I would surprise her if I could. But, as it turned out, she surprised me. Ruth Loving neither slept nor stayed inside. I wanted it to be a coincidence, Danny's mother standing on the front porch as I came up the walk, though I couldn't help but feel like she had been waiting for me. And maybe she had, for Danny's mother always had peculiar insight and feelings she claimed not to understand. And I was—reborn since the desert—much more open to her inclinations than I'd been in the past.

Ruth Loving stood tall and rail thin with blue eyes, like glass, and hair the color of a raven. Not a streak of gray lay in that black pool. And despite a few wrinkles at the corners of her eyes, her appearance belied her years. Her hair looked like it had been spun out of fine black metal strands, very regal, and cut in the pageboy style. She looked like a person out of a different era and she reminded me of a silent movie star whose name I could no longer recall.

Ruth was a lifelong smoker. Besides her marriage to Louis, nicotine was her longest running commitment. I was the only one who had never given her grief about it and she even suspected me of lifting a cigarette or two when I was younger. Danny had begged her to stop, as did Louis. She always responded in the same way and with the same tone and the phrase became her mantra. "I'll think about it," she'd say and smile and then take an extra-long drag. She'd let the smoke creep out in a breathless exhale. The act personified her defiant attitude.

The hour must have been incredibly early when Ruth headed out to the porch as judged by the pile of spent butts at her feet. I had not yet arrived so she stood there and smoked and bided her time. She was not prone to pacing. Instead, she expressed anxiety by holding her right arm across her body and tapping her left elbow. One hand held her cigarettes aloft, while the other tapped an incongruous beat against the hardest bone in her body. This activity greeted me upon arrival.

Ruth lit another cigarette and said, "I dreamed you coming here, this morning." The words escaped her in a whisper, accompanied by tendrils of smoke. She looked, briefly, like a dragon.

I stood before her at the bottom of the front steps. "I've seen his face in the dark, his eyes in the shadows," I said, and I fell to my knees. "He's coming for you."

"I know," Ruth said. "Now, if you'll excuse me, I'd rather not see this." And she went into her home and shut the door.

You'll die alone

I closed my eyes and put the gun barrel to my chest and pulled the trigger though not because of malice or madness. I've not been driven insane by what I've seen. No. But my debts had all been settled. Amends had been made in full.

And I wanted to go back to that darkness.

I wanted to see God again.

I wanted to see.

Nothing.

PART FOUR

On a crisp October day, Ruth Loving allowed an old fortune teller to take hold of her hand. She watched as the aged woman traced a line across her palm in such a way that caused a tickle in her navel and a lightness in her lower back. A sensation lost to her since learning to kiss without holding her breath, that youthful desperation to stretch innocent coupling into forever, though nothing lasts as long as eternity and the arousal, now, felt more like an open wound. Skin is rarely as exciting as it is before love becomes familiar to loss. She had tried forgetting James but he haunted her still.

And then, the psychic groaned and heaved sour bile at their feet. The elderly palmist collapsed. She died later that day. Such was the severity of Ruth's fortune.

Back at home, *her* home, Ruth relaxed with a book on the chaise lounge. She could not concentrate on the words and, soon, sentences ran together and pages became meaningless. The bay window overlooked the park across the street. Fall had burned away the color of the world. Leaves had long since fallen and been carried off by melodious winds to wherever dead leaves find final repose. Tree limbs took on the appearance of gnarled fingers reaching up in anger to throttle the traitorous sky and the sun that now refused warmth. Flowers on her son's grave had surely wilted. She no longer placed any at her husband's. Their union of convenience needed little in the way of memorial. Ruth wondered for whom she lived. She found solidarity with the trees. Life had burned away the color of her world. She stretched her fingers into the air.

But months would pass and those trees would teem with life and Ruth perceived this in herself. These very winds smelled of rain which promised to wash away her present grief. Nearby doves repeated a chorus reminding her that life existed as a series of cycles—of gates to walk through—like being forever ushered from one room to the next. A doctor once suggested, to her husband, that her happiness could be attained with a change of scenery. Ruth no longer recognized this life as her own. Change had arrived, though happiness still eluded her. And as long as James followed her through these gates, pursuing her from room to room, she would never feel the monstrous joy of a life lived for no one else. He made the rooms of her life into holding cells and punished her because she dared to deny his will. He thought himself special and, in that way, he shared the nature of so many men.

Ruth knew James would kill her. She saw it in her dreams and the fortune teller had read of it in Ruth's palm. He would arrive in but a few hours. She thought to prepare, to grab a weapon and defend herself, to write a letter, to say goodbye. None of it mattered, however. She could do all of it or none of it. Her dreams rarely lead her astray, so that is what she decided to do with the time left to her.

Ruth retired to her bedroom. She opened a drawer where a few of her secret things lived. An old letter sealed in an old envelope found a new home on the nightstand by the bed. She lowered the blinds and then crawled beneath the covers. Sleep came easy. Dreams did not lag far behind. Ruth sank into the deep. James was inevitable, after all, and inevitability offered its own relief. In that way, he was not unlike sleep and sleep was not unlike death. She wanted to enjoy the facsimile one last time. This would serve as her preparation for the real thing.

Then, something happened of which Ruth had not dreamed. She received an unexpected visitor. Ruth slept through the knocking and the doorbell hadn't worked in years. The pregnant girl who carried Daniel's child let herself into the home of Ruth Loving.

"Hello?" Rae called out. "It's me," she said, and she tiptoed past the empty living room and into the hallway.

The bedroom soaked in shadow, save the little bit of clarity creeping through the blinds. Errant glimmer of a nearby streetlight gave the interior a silver sheen. Rae did not dare turn on the overhead light. Rather, she cracked the door to the room ajar, so as to let in a little of the glow from the lamp in the hallway.

Rae barely opened her mouth when she said, "Ruth?"

This room faced south towards the street and to the park with the gnarled trees. The allowance was more or less a square, give or take a negligible measurement. The door opened at the northeast corner of the room, catty-corner to the bed. Lamplight cut the space in two and illuminated the open area in front of the footboard. Ruth slumbered in the middle of the large bed still draped in shadow. Two wooden chairs sat on either side of a chest of drawers against the wall to Rae's left. Pictures of the deceased hung in frames on the walls. This empty home struck the young girl as a type of sadness made manifest. Each room filled with reminders of a life that no longer existed.

Widow was another word for tragedy according to Rae's

father. The man expected Ruth to have received some amount of inheritance after the death of a husband and son and he thought to use his pregnant daughter as a kind of bait. She was not to return without reward, or at least the promise of some meager compensation.

"Ruth, it's me," she said. "It's Rae."

They had last spoken at the funeral. Ruth offered friendship to the young woman and an open invitation to be a part of her life. Rae accepted the offer through tears and they embraced. But they had not spoken since.

An invitation to Ruth's Victorian home sounded beautiful. More importantly, it was far away from Rae's father. He believed, however, that a good distance would help to facilitate a forgetting of Daniel. He did not wish to live with a hysterical woman, but as the impending costs of the baby loomed, the man began to scheme.

Rae said, "I'm sorry I never came to visit." She sat lightly on the edge of the bed. "I'm sorry I lied to you."

"I know," Ruth said in her sleep. The voice was so soft that Rae worried she'd imagined it. "I know," Ruth said, again, louder than before.

Ruth Loving sat up and looked right into Rae's eyes. "I know," Ruth said. She reached out and touched Rae's cheek.

Ruth smiled. The woman looked as though she received revelation. Her wide eyes peered in Rae's direction, though not at her. Ruth looked through the young woman and searched for an answer to her dream of doom. She saw a reversal of fortune.

Rae remembered Daniel and his ever-searching eyes. Ruth's eyes were practically the same. Eyes like blue ghosts. The idea caused her to shiver.

"I'm glad you've come," Ruth said. She stopped smiling. Her eyes narrowed and her brow furrowed. She squeezed Rae's hand. "I know," she said. The corners of her mouth pulled down into a deep frown. She cried and said, "I know."

Ruth started to shake. Rae pulled her close and held her in her arms. The heat of Rae's swollen belly radiated against Ruth's colder frame. It was not the forgetting that was painful. The pain lay in the remembering. Ruth pulled away from Rae. She seemed lost again, searching and smiling.

"I'll make us tea," Ruth said. She threw back the covers. "I hope you mean to stay for a bit," she said, and darted out of bed. "I could use your help," she called out as she made her way to the kitchen at the back of the house.

A photograph atop the dresser caught Rae's attention.

The frame was red and decorated in embossed hearts. In the photo, Ruth appeared much younger and had more length to her hair. She was smiling and had an arm around two young men who each held sparklers. The snapshot looked very much as though they attended a Fourth of July celebration. Rae recognized the younger Louis but not the other man. Perhaps, she wondered, their friendship ended tragically. Rae had only ever read about doomed love triangles. She suspected Louis had bested the stranger.

Rae turned and Ruth held out a steaming porcelain cup.

Rae said, "Thank you," and she took the drink. "It's very kind of you."

Ruth said, "Any day now?" She pointed to Rae's round stomach. "You pick out a name?"

"My daddy doesn't like the idea," Rae said, "but if it is a boy, I'll name him Daniel, and if it's a girl, she'll be Danielle."

"Well, I think that is lovely," Ruth said. "I appreciate that."

Rae said, "When my momma passed, daddy said he wished I didn't have her name. He won't call me Rachel. Never has. Not even when I'm in trouble." Rae turned away from Ruth and looked back at the stranger in the photograph. "Daddy's never been the same since momma," she said.

"A death will do that," Ruth said. She sighed and looked past the girl towards the picture in the red frame. "Nothing brings out the worst in people like death and love and money."

"You'd think people would be more"—Rae paused and felt a pang of guilt—"straightforward." She hated her father in that moment and wondered if she had always hated him.

Ruth sensed the girl's unease and wished to calm her. "Everybody's got secrets, young lady," she said. The web she spun filled with sincerity. The girl could not be allowed to leave.

"How come you're so nice to me?" Rae said. "What's in it for you?"

"Why," Ruth said, "absolutely everything." She walked across the room to the bed. "Can I tell you something?" She tucked sheets, and then fluffed the pillows. "And I don't mean it to be awkward," she said.

Rae waited for her to follow up, but the woman kept working, and Rae realized that Ruth honestly waited for permission.

"Tell me," Rae said. She sipped the coffee. "I promise I won't judge."

Ruth seemed to look at the floor but in her mind she cruised through distant memories. She said in a flat tone, "I wish Daniel's father had been a better man." She flattened the sheets with her palm and then stopped to lean on the bed. "Daniel," she said, "he was a good man. I raised him, taught him to defend himself, how to shoot, how to fish. He was a good man." She shook her head and looked up at Rae. "Good wasn't really what I'd use to describe his father," she said.

Rae looked over her shoulder at the framed photo. Young Louis held his sparkler and grinned. "He looked happy enough," she said. She no longer understood their conversation, though she thought she did.

"Oh, we had our pleasant times," Ruth said. "But they were few and far between in those last years. Before Danny came along."

"You know," Rae said. "Once this baby comes, I'm going to leave here. Nothing says you have to stay in this house, or the town, for that matter."

Ruth smiled, feeling most bemused. She said, "Where am I going to go?" She raised her eyebrows in anticipation of a response from her charge.

Rae remained mum.

Ruth said, "Even if I could get someplace, my cousins in Illinois, for instance, I am a widow with no work experience. I don't have the money to move. Klamath is my home. When I'm buried, it'll be next to my boy, thank you."

"I didn't mean to upset you," Rae said.

"I know you didn't," Ruth said. "And I'm not angry at you, just life. It's not fair."

"No ma'am," Rae said very quietly.

"There's a hot meal waiting for you in the kitchen." She started out of the room. "I'm sure you're itching to get out and about, but you ought to eat first. A proper meal is the least I can do to repay you for your unexpected company."

"I shouldn't have dropped in like this."

"Quite the contrary," Ruth said. "Most fortuitous if I'm being honest."

Rae sat at the table and Ruth served the young woman her meal. Then, Ruth left the room and returned a few minutes later. She handed Rae the envelope from the nightstand.

"What's this?" Rae said.

"I must step out of the house for a quick errand," Ruth said. She had to fight to control her shaking body and fight to keep from stammering. She coughed and brushed her hands down her front in an effort to compose. "There's a man coming by. Give him that note. He'll be on his way."

Rae flipped the envelope back and forth in her hand. "It looks old," she said. She traced the sloppy cursive on the front of the envelope with her finger and said, "Who is James?"

"I should have put that in the post ages ago, but I never did," Ruth said. "I could never figure out why I didn't send the letter, but now I know I was never meant to." Ruth tried to smile, but the overwhelming urge to cry made smiling impossible. She said, "Enjoy the meal." Ruth hurried out of the kitchen. The front door closed.

Rae never considered that a warm meal could be a trap. But the food tasted a sight better than anything she would have at home. Her father only knew how to boil and burn food. And this is how the impressionable and pregnant girl became bait for a second time in the same day.

About two miles away, James hiked down a side street towards the river. The banks smelled of stale water and damp mud. Sun set and colored the winding stream like an exposed vein. Rays of light reached up above the horizon and cut through distant clouds in desperate streaks of orange and red like a fire at the edge of the Earth. A pang of jealousy rippled through him. He would never burn as bright.

Darkness finally began to cast out illumination and James's eyes adjusted to the boom and glow of passing streetlights. Clothes soaked with sweat. Perspiration tickled his lower back and ran to his waistband. The collared shirt, once white but darkened to a wet grey, felt glued to his skin. The sensation of total body suffocation aggravated him. The fabric had an unnatural weight. Damp clothes were their own kind of prison.

James stood at the bottom of the hill. He stared up the long street towards the address Daniel had given him. Close, but still so far. Birdsong intermixed with distant traffic, the occasional solitary bark, and unintelligible conversations that carried out amongst the porches and the driveways of the Pacific Terrace neighborhood.

People smiled and waved at him. He would nod and hoped against hope that someone would see his effort and offer him a ride. But no one offered anyone a ride anymore.

Smiles and friendly waves were false prophets of geniality.

In the animal kingdom, barring teeth was a sign of aggression meant to ward off enemies. Human beings turned parted lips and teeth into their standard greeting, but it meant the same thing: *I am afraid of you and I am dangerous*. James cursed the friendly and unhelpful people in his mind as he passed them by, while offering up his own bared teeth.

Everything seemed uphill after so much travel. This last stretch, literally uphill, would no doubt feel like a gauntlet. He longed for a dry heat the way some people reminisce about spent youth.

James watched a dog play in a neighbor's sprinkler. The mutt shook, water arcing off the animal in splattering sheets. He had never envied a dog before.

Ruth's two-story Victorian loomed before him. His destination lay no further than the length of a walkway and a tall porch. He licked his lips and rubbed his hands together.

James had never actually stopped to consider a house. This one appeared quite beautiful, with its yellow siding and white shutters and red front door. The home projected a kindness, and kindness was inviting, and a relief. A grave for the living ought to be beautiful. The idea warmed his heart. He allowed himself to lose a moment or two to memories of faraway days.

He felt lucky that Ruth took a shine to him all those years ago. And he knew she had loved him. What kind of debt could justify her kindness?

Ruth, of course, would want to know what really happened to her son out in the desert.

Answers, James decided, were his debt to her. He would give her that, at least. When he owed her nothing more, he would take what he wanted and be on his way. He swelled with the idea of romance and imagined himself a knight about to slay a dragon that he loved but could not let live. She had cast a spell over him and he intended to break that spell. He would eat her heart if that is what it took to free him.

James walked through the intricate archway above the steps, with its fanciful designs and lattice work, and onto the porch. The screen door would not budge, so he tried pushing the doorbell with his elbow, but the button was too small. He used his knuckle. There was no sound. He crushed his knuckle into the doorbell, again, and there was nothing. He put an ear to the screen door.

He tapped the screen door with his shoe, turned, and nearly jumped out of his skin. What he'd thought to be a ghost was nothing more than a very pregnant young woman staring at him through the bay window. He smiled and motioned towards the front door. She smiled back and held up a finger.

The front door proper, a large wooden thing painted red, creaked open and the young woman stuck her head through the crack. "Are you here for the letter?" Rae said. She had the envelope clutched between her fingers.

"I'm here for something—say," James said. He sniffed the air coming from inside the home. "That smells awfully good."

"Miss Loving's a great cook," Rae said.

James leaned an elbow on the door frame and said, "Don't I know it. She happen to be home?" He patted his stomach. "I am starving," he said.

"She said I'd give you this letter and you'd be on your way."

James smiled and rested his forehead on the screen door and said, "She tell you that?"

"Yes, sir."

James whistled. "Well," he said. "You just pop open this screen door and I'll take what's mine, then." He tapped his fingertips on the frame.

"I don't like your tone, mister."

James said, "Hey now." He jumped away from the door with his hands up and he grinned. "Give me that letter," he said. "Me and my tone will be on our way. Just like Ruth told you."

"You saying Miss Loving's a liar?"

"Not directly," James said. "But I don't doubt she knows the value of a sacrificial lamb, especially one busting at the seams." James took another step backward and stuffed his hands into his pants pockets. He rocked on his heels. "Boy or girl?"

"I don't know, mister," Ruth said. His distance gave her a false sense of security and she took the opportunity. "Just take your letter and go," she said and opened the screen door just a hair's breadth. James had the handle in his hand before the letter dropped to the ground. She didn't even see him move.

"We used to raise beef cattle," James said. "Kept some heifers for milk and breeding but they eat like there's no tomorrow, so we killed most the females out the gate, so to speak. Raised the males and ate them. My father got so he could tell if the swollen heifers were having girls or boys. I thought he was full of stuffing but damned if he didn't get it right every time."

"Please let go, mister," Rae said, her voice a pitiful pitch.

"He'd stuff his arm clean up that cow's asshole. No glove and to the elbow. Said he could grab the uterus and feel the calf and he swore up and down that he knew what it was. Sexing the calf is what he called it." James laughed. "Suppose you don't mind me coming inside."

Rae held onto the handle so tightly and said through tears, "She said take that letter and go." Her hands were white. Sweat dotted her skin. She sobbed and pulled with all her might but he had such strength. She may as well have been a feather.

James snatched the letter and let himself in the house. Rae tried to run, but James grabbed a handful of hair and led her to the living room. He shoved the girl down onto the chaise lounge and said, "Move an inch and you'll never be a mother, so help me."

There had been a certain order to the things in Ruth's room when they were growing up. There was always an order, ever since she first suspected her mother and father of going through her belongings when she wasn't home. Ruth was a secretive child. They were curious parents. Now, James's turn to be curious had come at long last.

James had been careful to pay attention to the angles of notebooks and paper atop the console just inside the entry.

There were particular arrangements of books on her shelves. He wondered if she still laid a single hair across the switch of a desk lamp. As teenagers, even the clothes in her closet were separated in an order that, if tampered with, would have been alarming to her.

And nothing tattered or torn was ever kept by Ruth. She had no use for worn items. She lived like a snake that shed its skin every single day. Accumulation meant age and Ruth meant to live forever. She had been like that when they were very young and seemed to remain that way wherever she went, even in this house. Spartan best described the interior decor. Everything, top to bottom, looked new. You'd hardly believe anyone even lived here.

Knowing Ruth in this way, James felt shocked by the aged envelope given to him by the sobbing girl. He turned it over in his hand, a yellowed envelope, sealed, with no return address. Cracks ebbed from the corners. And his eyes welled with tears and he put a hand over his mouth.

She had written his name. Her penmanship was awful but no doubt the name was his. He could not recall the last time he received a letter. Post in the mountains invited a sense of novelty and few that knew James yet lived. But the lack of a return address bothered him. The information inside didn't warrant a phone call or any kind of visitation and Ruth obviously wasn't waiting for a response. Though, perhaps, there was a different reason for the anonymity. Regardless, the circumstances alerted James to one thing.

This letter contained secrets.

James sat on the floor and picked at the letter. He tapped it a couple of times against his mouth and worked at the corner until he chewed open a hole big enough to press his finger through.

He tore the envelope open and pulled the letter out. None of Ruth's poor handwriting graced the page. He had to settle for black typeface.

It read:

James,

A song about falling in love. The name of the song I no longer remember. You sang that song to me. Water rose above our shoulders and we floated between two worlds. Your embrace kept us both warm. Nothing like night swimming except for dreams in which we're flying. I dream of how you used to be and why I truly left you all those years ago. Daniel is your son, but I feared what you'd become. Life is what you make it, yes, though what life is made from is gifted to us by those who came before. The gifts you had to give terrified me. Terrified Louis, too, and he tried to give us safe passage. We took your mother's maiden name. She died when you were so young and Louis knew the name was lost to you. Your brother did his best by us, though his heart belonged to Elliot. Please, know I forgive you. You and I will always be next to that river. You, deep inside me, and I, wrapped around you, the way lovers do. Nothing else now matters. Memory remains. Please know I forgive you. I hope if you do meet Danny, this letter finds you first. He is all that lingers of our love we shared before. He is our moment at the river. See us in his eyes. He will love you in a way in which I am no longer able and he is part of your world. Let him in. And know that I once loved you enough to carry part of you inside me. So, this is how we part forever more, my riverside, my warm embrace, my nameless song. Please know that I forgive you. For all you have done or will ever do, I forgive you.

James dropped the letter to his side and let his hands rest in his lap. He stared out the bay window past the girl who cowered on the chaise lounge. Minutes passed. Not a cloud in the sky. Darkness settled and the west shimmered.

Rae barely managed a whisper. "Ruth said you could have that letter and that you'd be on your way."

"I tore my own son to pieces," James said. "Took him like a lover, ate his eyes while he was still alive, and then I choked him to death with the desert floor." James looked at Rae and smiled. "I'll take this letter, you're right about that—take this letter and whatever else I damn well please."

Rae barely moved her mouth and her words came out like a hum. "What do you want from me, Mister?" she said.

James crawled across the floor towards her. "Oblivion," James said. "Self-oblivion." He lay his head in her lap. "I no longer belong to mankind."

"Please don't kill me."

"It is not you I wish to kill," he said. "But I can neither plunge nor recede."

"Suicides go to Hell."

"Dear child," James said. "Where do you think we are?" He rose to his knees and kissed her and she trembled against him and her terror produced a slight sweetness in the taste of her salty tears. He grabbed her, a hand on either side of her face, forced her to meet his gaze, and said, "The rape of corpses drifting through this prison, this providence called life, are nothing more than judgment meted out in varying degrees by a divinity that is unfathomable, a void unsearchable and immaculate in its profundity." He wiped her cheek with his blood-stained thumb. "My desires turn like a wheel," he said, and then sighed. James let the girl go and she scrambled away from him and into the furthest corner of the room. James stood and pointed at her. He said, "If you see Ruth, let her know my sermon is finished, and I understand that which I have pursued all this time is simply my own destruction."

Rae said nothing. The pregnant girl bobbed her head and

trembled before the man she believed meant her death. She had felt fear of men before, but this gripped her in a way she did not, at first, comprehend. And then the baby kicked and her hands instinctively went to her swollen stomach. Rae felt fear, though not of her own bodily violation, but for the body trapped inside her. She knew she could not fight this man if it came to that, but she could hurt him. Her trembles ceased. She held very still and followed his movement using only her eyes.

James knew that look all too well. She meant to meet him head on. Prey rarely prostrated itself but would observe with steely reservation its own undoing. Stillness acted as preamble to the hymn of the damned. She did not need to sing for him and he had no use for her song. He imagined she would be a good mother, as long as she never forgot how to fear. He blew the girl a kiss and walked out of the house and onto the tall porch.

And now it was his turn to feel fear. James held very still. He observed his end.

Ruth waited at the bottom of the steps like an infernal god. James thought she walked with a cane until the weapon rose to meet him. A shotgun blast shredded his stomach and sent him backwards through the screen door and into the home. He teetered on the curve of his spine and screamed like any creature set upon by merciless nature. He cried. Hands hovered at his open cavity. Blood accompanied his guttural words.

"You said you forgave me," he said to the black silhouette at the door.

Death, then, walked inside and stood above him.

"There is no revenge so complete as forgiveness," Ruth said as she reloaded.

James grinned but did not have time to laugh.

The shotgun blast split James's head like ripe fruit. And then, though his eyes no longer existed, all the colors beyond human sight unfurled before him and the void was so beautiful, achingly so. The Gates of Nihil radiated light like a fire and shone the color of gemstones and nothing mattered any longer. James returned to Empyrean.

Ruth knelt beside the raw and ruined corpse of her lover. She held it in her arms and together they looked like *pietà* in a slaughterhouse. By a trick of the dim light within her home, all that blood blackened like water in moonlight. They were at the riverside again. But now, the only song about love was the beating of Ruth's heart.

James blossomed over everything he touched. How many times had Ruth seen these very blooms on her clothes and sheets and in the bath or in the fireworks on the Fourth of July or blood in a basin and even among the shooting stars? The entire universe and its creation and all of her memories converged in that single violent moment.

Ruth screamed but sang no hymn. Her pain offered no conversion. Death existed as a certainty unencumbered by belief and she refused its worship and triumphed against her own despair. A rush of nighttime breeze crossed her face as though a cell door had pulled open. She closed her eyes and walked through and welcomed her monstrous joy.

No face to meet her in that darkness. No eyes watched from the shadows. She gazed into the abyss. She saw *nothing*.

Ruth was free.

EPILOGUE

In the desert there is a beast roaming alone and quite mad. The beast believes truth to be held captive by its heart and that this truth excuses its actions. Violence being the action excused most frequently. But the terminus for all beasts is the same regardless of their hearts and all beasts wish to be the exception.

In void, beasts grow out of material culled from creation and are then thrusted into unforgiving light. A great din fills this interim. The cacophony soon becomes nemesis. Beasts combat this unpleasant noise with a tumult of their own making in an attempt to stave off madness. The discordance of beasts creates great shadows which loom over ages and ages until such a time as a mighty crescendo threatens to silence all. Noise recedes but the din always begins anew. Interpretations of this pandemonium are as numerous as the stars above. And the hearts of beasts clash with a fervor particular to desperate ego and vainglorious righteousness.

All beasts return to the void from whence they came.

Din will die along with light and shadows will become shadow.

This truth I hold captive in my heart.

ACKNOWLEDGMENTS

Many thanks to Karl and Whitney Fischer at Excession Press for taking this manuscript into their home and treating it as one of their own. All passion projects should be so lucky.

And, as always, thanks to: the beta readers; editors; my patient family.

Very special mention goes to Daniele Serra for his wonderful cover art and interior illustrations.

As well, it would be a shame if I did not thank Messrs. Kevin L. Donihe and Don Noble. The kernel for this book found life in our sleep-deprived conversations as we traveled cross-country in November of 2016. I am very thankful for our time in the desert, and pleased as punch that none of us were devoured by any of the wild ass that yet wanders some of the desolate corners of the United States of America. We did it, gents! Drinks all around . . .

Also, very special thanks to you, dear reader, for picking up this book and giving it a whirl. You are a diamond, truly.

Finally, to Phillip Bush, who may have been one of the most genuine human beings I have ever met. He was kind, and he was patient. I knew Phil for most of my life. We played baseball, as kids, and went to the same schools in the same little town. His enthusiasm for horror movies and TV shows and books kept us in touch, later in life. He was always very supportive, unfailingly so, and the man was as big a fan of the horror genre as I've ever known. Thanks, Phil. You are missed.

ABOUT THE AUTHOR

Nicholas Day resides in Southern Oregon with his family. He studied at Southern Illinois University and Seton Hill University. Previously published works include two novellas and two short-story collections, including the Wonderland Award-nominated collection Now That We're Alone and the nominee for This Is Horror's "Novella of the Year," At the End of the Day I Burst into Flames.

Grind Your Bones to Dust is his first novel.

Find him at nicholasdayonline.com

CPSIA information can be obtained
at www.ICGtesting.com
Printed in the USA
LVHW091034021019
632709LV00011B/821/P

9 781733 990134